THE THICKEST SOUP YOU'VE GOT

Nikki R. Leigh

SLASHIC HORROR
PRESS

Other titles by Nikki R. Leigh

Lessons in Demoralization
Her Teeth, Like Waves

Originally published in Australia by Slashic Horror Press in 2024.

SLASHIC HORROR
PRESS

ISBN: 978-0-9756380-5-7
Cover design by Christy Aldridge of Grim Poppy Designs
Interior design by Cat Voleur
Edited by David-Jack Fletcher

Introduction: A Cooking Lesson

You open an Internet browser to find a recipe to do something with that pack of beef you bought two weeks ago. You're certain it's only a day away from rotting, and you can't stand the fetid smell that will permeate throughout your kitchen and absorb into the cold plastic in your fridge if you leave it to sit.

What can I do? you think, wracking your brain for what spices exist in your drawers and what vegetables aren't yet wilted in the ceramic bowl on your counter.

You browse and click through blogs and websites, searching for something, anything to use up what's left in your cupboard.

Your eyes fall on a link. You click it, and scowl at the white text on a black background and backtrack. You'll be damned if you're going to allow the dark mode site to wreak havoc on your vision, even if that stroganoff looked amazing.

You're about to give up and just cook the beef to put in a bowl to be eaten with some ketchup and a spoon when a recipe catches your eye. You blink at the title, thinking that can't possibly be correct. But there it is, the dish's name in bolded Comic Sans font at the top of the page.

Death Beef.

You read on, nearly squealing in joy when you see just how easy the steps are to follow. You figure that the cook behind this must be really into death metal and being hardcore in all parts of their lives, and don't give the title another thought. You're just happy that you found a way to get rid of so many things in your pantry before their expiration date, a feat you rarely accomplish.

A dash of salt. *Maybe another pinch, for good measure*, you think.

Two egg yolks, beaten into submission.

Chopped parsley.

Boiled spaghetti noodles.

Three cloves of garlic.

A drop of blood.

Wait. That can't be right. You wonder if this is just Edgy-EdgeLord-just having a laugh. You're cutting an onion, debating adding the drop in case it really was necessary for the dish. The knife makes the decision for you, nicking the side of your finger, blood welling at the site of the skin flap. You let a droplet of blood fall into the pan, just for fun. It sizzles and thickens.

You follow the steps, one after another. You break a sweat doing the dance it describes. Bite your cheek trying to speak the words the recipe demands you chant at the boiling pasta. A tear drips from your eye as you force yourself to cry, thinking about the saddest cat you saw on social media last week. The tear falls into the sizzling sauce, smoking from the pan on the stove.

Just a few more minutes and the dish will be done. Then you can take it on your lap tray to the couch and the television, the latest episode of your favorite wrestling show calling your name. You tap your foot, growing impatient as you realize you don't know what "thick enough" sauce looks like. You wait down the last ticking seconds on the timer.

Finally, you plate your meal, enjoying the glistening fat on the beef and the savory scent of the noodles and sauce. You're not much of a chef, but you're proud of what you created.

Plunking yourself onto the couch, you turn the TV on. As the opening announcer riles up the crowd for the first fight, you plunge a bite of Death Beef and noodles into your mouth.

You chew, your teeth mashing the tender beef into a fine puree. You let the noodles and sauce slide over your tongue, groaning into your fork. You're so enraptured by the delicious bites you take, one by one, you don't even care that your favorite wrestler just got cheated by a jobber. Before you know it, the first match ends with a loud bell rung and your plate is empty.

You're devastated. You know it's a disproportionate reaction to the realization that the most amazing meal of your life is over, but the pain wells up anyway, like a tidal wave of hot anger that boils like magma in your gut.

And that's when the vomiting begins. The best thing you've ever cooked makes a second appearance, and it doesn't stop when it's all out. Your body doesn't have any food left to give, but the cramps and heaves continue, unaffected by your sobs.

You can't possibly have expected what happens next, but you swear you see bones in the next wave of refuse that bubbles up from your stomach. The beaks of birds follows; the hooves of cows and pigs comes soon after. You're throwing up every animal you've ever eaten from the bottomless pit you've become. The living room smells like rot and ruin.

After hours of regurgitating pound after pound of each ounce of meat you've consumed in your thirty years as a proud omnivore, you lie in your refuse, fading out to blackness.

Your heart beats rapidly, then slows, then stops.

The last thing you hear is the laughter of gods, the roiling of their guffaws like the waves of the ocean, filling you with one final thought.

The vegans were right.

Recipes found online are filled with cautionary tales. Their authors lament about their own lives, forcing you to scroll to halfway down the page just to figure out what ingredients you need. You'd think with all the advances we've made in food production and distribution, with creating and cooking and sharing our love for all things edible we'd have seen it all.

This book brings you the untold. The provoked blade of the culinary world fighting back to remind us that with food comes pain. The death of something else. The labor and sweat and blood and tears of those that produce.

Inside you'll find unhinged chefs, untapped food sources in the deepest, darkest corners of Earth and in space. You'll heat things with tales of greed, of love, of systematic transgressions. Of mystery and gods and the perils of media. Of exploration and family and dishes best served cold.

I hope you like the taste of iron.

Open wide, and don't forget to chew.

Contents

Chapter 1
Signature Dish

From Culin-Nary a Care, December 21st

I spent my first evening at Guarigione—Chef Arlen's overnight sensation in the heart of West Hollywood—in tears. And no, thank you for your condolences, but I myself haven't encountered any recent traumas. My life at home with Laurel has been as good as ever. Just the other night we adopted a cat. The little tortie seemed to love to twist herself up, just like fusilli pasta, so that became her name. Fusilli. She's fast becoming Laurel and my favorite little noodle.

So, see? No trauma, no sadness, no reason to sob into my plate of farfalle and blackened chicken. Yet, last Saturday, I and every other patron of Guarigione were dampening our plates with tears, grief heavy in our chests as we ate through Chef Arlen's most recent headliner. I know I'm supposed to use my power as a food critic to make it feel as though you can taste every last morsel of his dish, but I can only tell you that each tidbit of that plate made me mourn a grandmother I never had.

Guarigione on a Saturday was full. A line outside wrapped around the building. Inside, people hunched over their plates of food, arms cradling the rims of their white dishes as if attempting to hug the contents. They ate, bringing slow, dainty bites to their mouths, preserving the flavor, the memory. The diners caught their tears with their crisp white cloth napkins, not wanting to taint the flavor with their salt.

Without realizing it, I was doing the same. I'd forked mouthfuls of the farfalle and chicken into my mouth, the creamy sauce dripping with mushrooms and roasted garlic. Before I knew it, the food had taken me on a journey beyond the flavor train in my mouth.

The adventure started in a place of love. Child-like feelings of safety. The chicken reminded me of Quackers, a small hen I never owned. I almost swear, as the moistness of the roasted meat dripped down my chin, that I could remember the way a small child I've never seen— would chase her around a farm I've never been to. I could hear Not-Grandmother telling me to knock it off from the steps of her small house, apron cinched around her waist. The notes of pecan enriched the white meat, and I could smell the pie she cooked every winter.

The farfalle itself was the embodiment of Not-Grandmother's home—warm, inviting, just begging for you to stay—so much so that I spent precious minutes scraping what little remnants of sauce I could find with my fork. The horrible squeals of metal on ceramic repeated throughout the restaurant, suggesting the rest of the diners were doing the same.

I turned my attention, finally, to the arugula salad soaked in a sweet vinaigrette, forgotten when the first aromatic breeze of meat and pasta met my nose. I was glad I saved it for last, as the first bite of the damp, but still crisp salad hit my mouth, and my stomach turned to knots when I remembered Not-Grandmother's wake. The way I could only eat a salad, flavored with a dressing culled from her ingredients in her garden, because everything hurt too much. My Not-Grandmother, the matriarch and heart of the family, may she rest in peace.

Or "Rest in Peach" I heard her say in my mind, recalling how she wished to be buried under her favorite peach tree.

And that was where the journey ended. A brief serenade through a childhood I'd never lived, happiness, fulfillment, and then, as the dish ended, grief. All of this, a lifetime of memories of a woman I never met, in one night at Guarigione.

I've always heard a well-cooked meal is a story being told, but I've never actually played out scenes of a life that wasn't mine while eating. It was magical. It was terrifying.

The food was delicious, satisfying, dripping with flavor. But the experience. The *experience*...

I have to go back.

***

"I'm telling you, Laurel, the place was like a dream. Or nightmare. I don't really know," Christina says, her elbows on the table, hands propping up her head, curly hair a curtain around her face.

"Everyone was just...crying?" Laurel asks, a hint of disbelief in her voice.

"Me included. It was like a scene out of a Wes Anderson movie. Surreal, but just kind of taken for granted."

"And you remembered your grandmother?"

Christina sighs. "Not my own. My grandma was a right old bat who hated us all. This grandmother, she was basically a *Better Homes & Gardens* magazine. Country edition. I ate Chef Arlen's dish and mourned a grandmother who was not mine."

"I think I need to see this for myself." Laurel is resolute.

Christina hops from the table and wraps her arms around her girlfriend's waist. "Date night?" she asks, her head resting on the taller woman's shoulder.

"Date night," Laurel confirms. Fusilli meows at their feet, weaving through their legs, and Christina feels whole in that moment.

The pair had been together for six years. Christina had never had a relationship like it before. She shared everything with Laurel—everything she could, at least. There were still some things Christina preferred to keep buried deep down.

One thing the two truly shared was a common love for food. Christina had started her food blog, Culi-Nary a Care, hoping to dine her way through West Hollywood. It began as an excuse to eat decadent meals all in the name of exploration, but it didn't take long until she established herself as one of the most followed food critics in the area.

Laurel is something of a chef herself, so Christina felt lucky to have a partner with a wholehearted acceptance of her food-based career.

Within a week, Christina is once again at Guarigione's, this time with Laurel at her side. Christina made reservations, using her minor celebrity status to sneak them into to the otherwise booked-solid restaurant. The smell of buttery prime rib had their mouths watering as soon as they step into the elegant dining room.

Laughter fills the air, some light chuckles, some loud roaring, and throughout their wait for the meal, Laurel and Christina almost have to shout to be heard.

"I can't believe we're here!" Laurel says, excitement in her eyes. Christina nods back at her, feeling her own glee bubbling inside. Since the two had made the reservation, the buzz surrounding the restaurant had only grown louder. Chef Arlen had prepared a new dish that had the local critics raving: the "Jane Bryant", named after a local comedian who'd recently had a successful tour. Every social media post she read described it as "gleeful" and oddly enough…"funny".

Christina breathes in the powerful scent of rosemary before placing a bite of steak in her mouth. The deep flavors bring forth a wave of emotions. The feeling of success, of evoking joy into people, overwhelms her. With each bite, she feels the satisfaction of sold-out crowds roaring with laughter, wiping tears from their eyes.

As she lifts a forkful of mashed potatoes into her mouth, she's nine, and she's just told her first joke. Her mother rewards her with a bite of buttery potatoes, laughing at her child's wit. Christina feels the need bubble inside in her, the desire to stop at nothing to make people laugh.

Every bite after is a punchline, calling forth fits of giggles from Christina. She can tell Laurel is experiencing the meal the same way, covering her open mouth as laughs erupt from her core.

She's beautiful when she laughs like that, Christina thinks.

Her plate is empty, but her heart is full.

***

From Culin-Nary a Care, January 2nd

Since my last post, we've been to Guarigione's twice more. We're becoming regulars there, despite the difficulty of re-booking. After Laurel and I ate the prime rib in near silence—save for the raucous laughter we couldn't contain—Laurel has made it her mission to make it to Guarigione's once a week.

I'm not sure if my ability to secure us reservations will last much longer, but I'm going to try to keep getting us in.

The Jane Bryant prime rib signature dish was perfection. A simple meal of steak, potatoes, and asparagus, was elevated by the emotion put into it. I've never been so happy while eating—or ever, come to think of it. I'm lucky neither of us choked, laughing through the meal at jokes that never left our lips.

Chef Arlen has a gift. Those first two meals, I truly felt something, and it was clear everyone who ate it felt the same way. Deep sadness, longing, and love with the farfalle, then like every funny bone in our bodies was struck with prime rib.

The third time we ate at Guarigione's, it all changed. I'm a bit concerned Laurel is spiraling into a spot of obsession, trying to understand how Chef Arlen's done it. How, with our last meal of clam chowder soup, we felt like we had discovered the key to unlocking ourselves. This time, the memory felt familiar, like the time I realized I was gay, that I felt a stirring in my loins.

And don't worry, I'm not about to start writing smut in the middle of my food blog. But let me tell you—that first bite of clam chowder felt like sexual freedom, discovery. Like strolls down a marina in San Francisco with my first lover's hand held in mine. Like a teenager in the 1980s careening down Lombard Street on a pair of roller skates on a dare, stomach flipping the whole way to impress the boy he was with. Like a middle finger to the crowd of onlookers as we kissed for the first time.

Laurel lost it when she finished her bowl, her cheeks flushed red.

I understood. I knew she needed to figure out how a bowl of clam chowder tasted like a sexual revolution.

And I did too.

***

"Did you see the news about Jane Bryant?" Laurel asks.

"You mean how the whole city is buzzing about the dish from a couple weeks ago?" Christina replies from her place on the couch, cup of coffee held in her hands.

"No, the actual comedian. She's missing."

Christina cranes her neck to watch Laurel banging about in the kitchen, setting up for her new recipe. "Missing?"

"Yeah, apparently for a week now. No one's heard from her. Missed a bunch of shows."

"That's awful. I hope she turns up. It seemed like her career was really taking off. I wonder if Chef Arlen will bring her dish back to raise awareness or something. Like a tribute."

"A tribute? She's not dead, Christina."

"You know what I mean. Anyways, I guess we'll find out tomorrow night. He's debuting another new dish and I managed to score us reservations."

Laurel shrieks in surprise. "Seriously, Christina? God, you're the best. I really wish we could talk with him. I want to cook like him. I want to make people *feel*. What are the odds we could go back to the kitchen? Meet the man behind it all?"

Rubbing the back of her neck, Christina's eyebrows furrowing in thought. "I don't know, babe. I've never seen him in the restaurant. He keeps a pretty low profile from what I've heard."

She observes Laurel's face, falling from its happy height when she realized she might never meet the masterful chef. Christina hates seeing that look on her face. Hates seeing her down. Laurel was the only person she was devastated to disappoint. It was part of why she never told her about her family's past, her sister's death.

Laurel knows Christina doesn't have a lot of family left. But if she ever found out why... Christina didn't think she would be able to recover. As it was, the anniversary of her sister's death is nearing, bringing horrible memories to the surface that she wishes she could fight back.

Every couple has secrets, right?

"I'll email the restaurant. See if we can do something. I want to make this happen for you."

Laurel's eyes light back up.

"We'll just have to make them notice us." Christina looks at Laurel's bright smile, melting inside. "Should be easy, with how beautiful you are."

She punches Christina lightly on the shoulder. "You're so corny." She gives her a gentle kiss on the lips. "But I love you."

***

At Guarigione's, Christina feels like she just can't quite get comfortable in her skin tonight. Perhaps it's the date, almost the hour on the dot when her house caught fire fifteen years earlier and her sister burned to death. Perhaps it's that she was suffering alone, unwilling to let Laurel in on the darkest corner of her past.

Perhaps it's something else.

Maybe that in the three meals she'd had at Guarigione's, she's grieved, she's laughed until she cried, and she's felt a sexual awakening. Maybe it's that she's felt these things that are not hers, yet with every bite became a part of her history. Maybe she is unsure of what tonight's dish will bring, and maybe that scares her.

She won't let Laurel see her nerves, because she seems to be vibrating with excitement, jittery in her seat. Like her lips are teeming with secrets she can't wait to spill.

"I'm just hoping we'll get to meet him," she says to Christina. A partial truth, to be sure. Laurel is excited to be able to have a chance to meet her newest idol. To pick his brain so she could cook as successfully as he. There is a little extra buzz about her veins because of the small box in her pocket. The tiny jewelry tucked inside that she kept telling herself isn't just a gimmick, isn't just to get his attention. It's to make her girlfriend happy. And if it *did* happen to catch Chef Arlen's eye?

The two chatted throughout their wait, sipping wine of deep red, smelling the aroma of baked salmon. The special dish for the night was called "Man's Best Friend". Every diner cast longing stares at their plates while eating, tears rimming their eyes, letting out short laughs.

Their plates arrive. Christina gives Laurel's hand a little squeeze, a brief "I love you" before forking a glistening piece of salmon into her mouth. Immediately, she's transported to the middle of a meadow, a lumpy furry shape at her side. As she takes another bite, she can see herself throwing a ball into the flowers, the shape revealing itself to be a dog, who darts after the thrown sphere. She fights the urge to yell out "Come here, girl!", hears Laurel whisper that same phrase under her breath, chewing the pink fish.

The lemon notes transport Christina to a darker place, fighting back tears as she remembers the death of a brother she never had. She feels herself wrap her arms around the German Shepherd, who rests her triangular head on her shoulder, poofing out air before licking her cheek.

The garlic—roasted to that perfect softness—lingers on her taste buds, and she laughs, recalling how her dog tries to fit her oversized body into her lap.

Across the table, Laurel is smiling to herself, trying to stop her hand from petting a dog that isn't there.

The two continue their ghostly serenade, the meal calling forth images they've never lived through. The salmon is devoured easily enough, the moist flaking and bright seasoning making the protein beautifully buoyant in their mouths. The Brussels sprouts are flavored with a complex array of spices and paired well with the decadent, brown herb rice, buttery and soft. All laced with memories of the sweet dog they don't own.

Their stomachs full, their brains humming with pleasant memories, Christina and Laurel shift back in the chairs, letting out breaths they'd been holding throughout the meal. Christina's hand rests on her stomach, rubbing her full belly.

The waiter comes around to their table, and Laurel requests a glass of red wine.

Christina's eyebrow raises in question. "Wine? Aren't we just about done here?"

Laurel stands up, confusing Christina further. When Laurel drops to one knee, pulling out a ring, Christina's world spins.

She barely hears the words Laurel is stuttering. Something about a life together, and being the perfect pairing of wine and food, but the speech warbles in and out as Christina reels from it all.

Her girlfriend. Her perfect girlfriend asking her for marriage, and all she can think about is how this day is already reserved for the memory of her sister's death.

But she knows, *she knows,* god she knows that she wants this with Laurel. Before Laurel gets the wrong idea and doubts her actions, Christina fumbles out a "Yes" and the two embrace. The restaurant grows loud with applause, congratulating the young couple, only adding to the cacophony in Christina's head.

Laurel slips an elegant ring on her finger, wipes her eyes with her dinner napkin, which had fallen to the floor in her escapades.

Laurel returns to her seat, grabs Christina's hand, and the two stare into each other's eyes. A moment of perfect romance despite the ugly parts they had both kicked under the same rug, doomed to lump together in the darkness.

Christina wishes she could erase the image of her sister's charred skin from her mind.

Laurel fools herself into thinking the proposal was made out of love.

Their waiter appears again, full glasses of wine on his tray. He places the maroon-filled glasses before them.

"Congratulations, you two," he says. "The chef would like to personally give you his regards. He says to bring the wine." The waiter nods toward the door beyond the restrooms. "Follow me."

The couple exchanges glances, excitement erasing their secret shames, and they tuck in their chairs and walk to the door.

They knock, and the door creaks open. Chef Arlen steps into view. He's shorter than Christina thought he would be. His gray mustache twinkles under the harsh lights, and his eyes bore into hers.

"Welcome, Christina and Laurel. Please, please, come into my office." His deep voice rumbles in his chest. "Congratulations on the grand moment. You had my restaurant feeling emotions I hadn't planned on them experiencing, but it was beautiful, nevertheless."

Christina wonders if they'd somehow pissed him off. Was he happy for them? Or angry?

Before she could clarify, Laurel steps forward and almost bows at Chef Arlen. "Chef, I'm a huge fan. I'm a cook, and I'm trying so hard to learn the craft. I've never tasted anything like what you do. You're such an inspiration and, oh jeez, I'm totally rambling but I just didn't think this would work—rather, I'd get a chance to meet you. I have so many questions."

Chef Arlen chuckles. "How about I show you? Please, finish your wine and relax."

The pair swirl their wine and down it, eager to chat with Chef Arlen. The celebratory wine down their throat, into their bloodstreams.

Christina feels hot. Heavy. Like a blur in time. Chef Arlen's figure wavers. The room is black. She falls.

***

In the restaurant basement, walled off, soundproofed, beneath the rug of Chef Arlen's office, Christina and Laurel wake up. Their heads throb, vision fuzzy, bodies buzzing. Christina opens her eyes, blinking away the static, almost sobs when she sees Laurel bound to a metal chair in front of a table. She feels her own bindings tight on her wrists and feet. The chair is rooted to the cement floor.

Their mouths are left free, a small mercy.

"The happy, newly engaged couple. What a fine dish you'll make."

Laurel's head lolls around her shoulders.

"Don't eat us, please," she stutters.

Chef Arlen laughs, a booming noise that ripples through Christina's aching head. "Eat you? In a sense sure, but not how you think." He reaches forward, lifting Laurel's chin. "You're beautiful, aren't you?" He nods back to Christina. "Quite lucky to have this one propose. So happy you'll get to spend the rest of your lives together, no matter how short that might be."

Christina shudders. How could this night, one filled with magic and wonder and love, end up in this dank basement? Looking around, she realizes the room is an elaborate kitchen, filled to the brim with produce and meats, an oven and stove, cookware and gadgets. Under better circumstances, she knows a place like this would be Laurel's dream.

Chef Arlen walks to the pantry, pulls out several dishes that look familiar to Christina. The chef points to the first dish, the blackened chicken and farfalle from Christina's first visit. "'The Violet', named after my grandmother."

He gestures toward the "Jane Bryant" prime rib and mashed potatoes, then to the clam chowder. "A favorite of mine: 'San Francisco skyline'."

Next to it, their dinner tonight: "Man's Best Friend".

"You've tried these four dishes of mine. Four of my best. Lucky you. I've no doubt the flavors are wonderful, but what you experienced when you ate. Surely, that's Michelin star worthy, no?"

He takes a bite of the "Jane Bryant", chuckles when he does.

"Food therapy. A way to eat your feelings before they eat you. All of my plates, my creations, represent a most special signature dish. A B-roll of footage cut from the lives of the most human people I've met. Would you like to meet the models?"

He doesn't wait for them to answer and walks away toward a closet. Christina's mind is blank, unsure of how to take any of this in. Laurel is slowly becoming more aware of her surroundings, and when she does, the guilt shadows her face. Christina doesn't understand why she'd look so guilty, it's not like she planned it—

And it strikes Christina that maybe she did.

"Laurel?" she whispers. "The proposal?"

Her fiancé is silent until she squeaks out a soft, "I'm sorry."

Chef Arlen returns, rolling a rack of what looks like four suit bags.

"Ladies, ladies. Save the drama for later when I'm peeling back your layers. Show a little respect to the models who sacrificed so much for a good meal."

He unzips the bags, one by one. He grips the contents of the first, placing it on the table in front of them.

Christina screams. Laurel vomits.

Before them, the withered skin of an old woman stares back from eyeless sockets. The skin is shriveled, like every organ and bone has been drained from the body, leaving behind a rubbery shell.

"My grandmother, Violet. My first signature dish. A mixture of my memories and hers. I learned from her that I needed the memories to be her own. Let her speak for herself. I tainted her memory with mine, and the resulting tears really diminished the plate."

He places in front of them three more skin suits.

"Jane Bryant, famous comedian. My first love, Jasper, model for 'San Francisco Skyline'. And my former sous chef, Mike. Oh, how he loved that dog. All honest. All themselves, for me and the plate."

The sounds of Laurel's gags trigger a similar reaction in Christina. She bites back bile as Chef Arlen continues.

"They've experienced so much, I just had to expose it. Such rich lives that make for the perfect ingredients. Figuring out what food represents their most memorable moments is a true joy, a true craft. You are what you eat, but you eat what they are. They gave me everything they were made of, and just like a good lobster, we had to leave the shells behind."

Laurel finds her voice. "What do you want with us?"

Chef Arlen fishes a small device from his pocket, then places the recorder in front of them all.

"I want your lives. All the details. Leading up to this moment, this joy of the proposal. When I saw you make your move, and the way the crowd reacted, I knew that moment needed to be cemented in culinary history. I've never modeled a couple before, but something tells me you have a lot to offer. Who should we start with?"

The air is heavy with hesitation. Christina wonders if this isn't some kind of awful kismet, that on this day, almost down to the hour, her story is demanded by a madman. Her eyes meet Chef Arlen's, volunteering herself.

"Start from the top," he demands.

She tells him of her childhood, growing up with her sister, their family bird. The moment she realized she was into girls. That she cheated on her exams in high school under intense pressure from her family. The way the sun caught her little sister's curly hair, and the giggle that followed her. She realizes Laurel is hearing some of this for the first time, the topic of her family avoided in an attempt to swallow down the guilt and shame of the actions that led to her sister's death.

Chef Arlen hangs onto every word, pulling ingredients from shelves as she speaks. He's a blur, moving so fast that the table seems to buckle under the weight of the mountain of food.

While the table fills, Christina feels herself deplete. Her words are heavy on her tongue, memories becoming more difficult to pull from their enviable black hole that Christina wishes she too could crawl into.

"Don't stop!" Chef Arlen yells. "Be my muse. Be my dish. Tell me what defines you. Give your story your signature." He barks orders, demanding more when her words grow thin. Christina fights against the memory she wants so badly to suppress.

The memory that has forced itself into her mind all day, on the anniversary of her sister's death. The anniversary of the fire that ripped sisters apart. That created the cloud of guilt raining on Christina's head.

She's never said any of what was about to come out of her mouth to anyone. Her parents believed the lie. She'd told it to others and herself enough that she almost believed it too.

"There was a fire," she murmurs. Chef Arlen stops his rummaging, his attention glued on her. She takes a breath. "I was babysitting my sister. She was asleep. It started in my room, from a candle I knocked over. I got out. My sister didn't."

Silence.

"Christina..." Laurel starts, having found her humanity.

"Shut up," Chef Arlen spits out. "More," he says to Christina.

"That's it. She died. Eight years old. I was fifteen. My parents never forgave me, and they shouldn't have."

"But how did you feel?"

"How the fuck do you think?" Her voice cracks. "How do you think I felt, knowing I'd killed my sister?"

"But you didn't. It sounds like it was just an accident," Laurel says.

Christina remembers the way her sister reached for her from her room, behind a wall of fire. How she trembled in place, frozen by the flames. How she said nothing as she turned away and barreled out the door, too scared to cross the fire, leaving her sister to burn.

"It was an accident," Christina whispered.

She didn't say another word for the next hour, and Chef Arlen respected her wishes. He had gotten what he wanted from her. An emotion he had yet to model. A life he had yet to preserve. He decides he doesn't even need the couple angle.

He presents the dish to Laurel. A grilled duck breast with a spicy orange sauce on a zesty rice pilaf.

"Eat it," he says. She looks almost delighted to sample his prototype. Her arms still bound, Chef Arlen dangles a bite from a fork in front of her face, which she consumes, eager to taste his creation. With the first bite of flavor, bursting, burning through her, her eyes light up. The flavor, so rich. It tastes like the passion of a lie. Like a secret on the tip of the tongue. A happy life, burned away in a moment.

Chef Arlen forks bite after bite into her open mouth, not waiting for her to swallow before jamming another inside. Laurel tastes it all, smiling until she isn't. Her mouth full of duck, her face turns to panic. She spits the food out, chunks tumbling down her chin.

Chef Arlen smiles as Laurel's skin begins to crackle. Her hair curls and smokes, her eyes almost bursting from the internal heat. He knew Christina would be a dish most special. He had cracked the recipe at last.

Laurel's face begins to droop, and the screaming starts. Christina gags at the scent of burning flesh, watching as Laurel's skin turns to a crisp and blackened layer, melting away just like she imagined her sister's to have fifteen years ago.

Christina watches her lover burn, and she feels nothing. She can't even feel the relief of someone finally knowing the darkest part of her life.

She says nothing, another rash of silence following a tragedy. She slouches as her bones begin to dissolve, as her organs turn to soup. Chef Arlen has taken it all, leeched his model dry as she feels her own insides falling out of her, leaving her to deflate into another skin suit for Chef Arlen's collection. Remnants of his inspiration.

Chef Arlen smiles.

Christina's signature dish would light the world on fire.

Chapter 2
Why I Hate Legends, But Love My Mom and Sea Weed

Mly mom is a piece of shit.

No wait, I don't mean that. I love her, I do. But right now, I'm teetering on the edge of a mental breakdown and it's her fault.

She couldn't have known, but she also totally should have. I mean, she's aware that my anxiety has been through the roof the last few years. That's why she was trying to get me out of the house.

And that's how I ended up here, at this live studio taping for *Myths of the Forgotten Sanctuary*. How this adult game show, based on some kid shit from back in the day, got to be a success eludes me. I don't know, guess they thought it would be funny to see adults climbing on their hands and knees, making fools of themselves as they weave their way through a maze trying to find ancient keys to get them out of the jungle. Or castle. Or whatever the set designers have rigged that's mildly culturally appropriative.

Fucking adult-ass McDonald's PlayPlace is what it is.

But people love it.

My mom loves it.

And so now, I'm a member of this live audience, to watch adults with minimum wage jobs try to supplement their way of life by looking like idiots on live television. I look over at my mom, already sitting on the edge of her seat. She's got her bright pink "I found my way through the Forgotten Sanctuary and all I got was this T-shirt" on, and there's a big grin on her face.

She's not a total piece of shit. As weird and annoying as she can be, I do love her.

The place is filling up with other viewers, their smiles all as wide as Mom's. The lights on the stage are so bright, I swear they're going to trigger a migraine. And with the arriving audience comes the plethora of...smells. Perfume, body odor, food. They all mix together in a tangle of something that smells like diabetes—that horrid, sickly-sweet sweat that lingers in the air like toxic humidity. We've not long been here and already I can feel my anxiety banging and banging on the roof, threatening to tape a rocket to its ass and burst right through.

I promised Mom I wouldn't light up before the show. I promised her I'd do my best to get through it.

But sometimes you have to do the things that might disappoint your parents a little, so you don't disappoint them even more by getting so anxious you just bolt out the door and call an Uber home.

"Going to unload, a little," I say.

"Right now, Martha?"

"Choose your lane, Mom. Either I can stay hydrated, or I can avoid public restrooms. Can't have them both."

She squints her eyes at me, the beginnings of her best Mom Glare.

"Better now than in the middle of the taping. I promise I'll be back before you know it." A promise I can actually keep. I give Mom's hand a little squeeze, grab my purse, and head to the bathroom, right to the big stall, closest to the tiny open window. Then I drop my jeans, take a seat, and rifle through my purse for the tiny bit of salvation I know is in there. Finally, my fingers find the pen-shaped vessel at the bottom of my purse, and I sigh in relief. I'd left it in there after all this time, just in case.

I tap the vape on, bring it to my lips, and suck with all my might. It takes a minute to get it warmed up, but when it finally clears and that light turns green on the other end—

Salvation.

Tastes a little different than I remember. It might be a little stale, but that cloud of weed hits my lungs, and even if it's not working its magic quite yet, my body acts like it's already pulsing through my veins. That's some CBD love, right there, uncoiling all the taut parts of my body. I only keep the stuff with little to no THC in my purse, so I don't make an ass out of myself when the psychoactive bits come into play. Just a nice little hum in my body. A little pillow for my brain.

I make my way back to the set and slouch into my seat.

Mom crinkles her nose. "Martha, seriously?"

I know it's a lost battle. "Just be glad I'm here, Mom."

She sighs again, narrowing those eyes back into The Glare™ and I start going into overdrive wondering if she'll ever get over the fact that her daughter is a) gay and b) a frequent weed user, thanks to the debilitating mental health issues her family passed onto me. It's her fault, really.

I don't have much time to spiral into oblivion when the lights start to flicker, indicating the beginning of the taping. Within seconds, a hush falls over the crowd and the host Dirk Dog waltzes onto stage.

His eyes sparkle under the lights, and I see Mom shudder under his smoldering stare.

"Oh, isn't he just the most handsome?" Her lips purse. "I mean, I guess he's not your type."

I try to ignore the disappointment in Mom's voice. "I'm sure you can dazzle him later at the meet and greet. He makes Dad look like a slice of bologna."

"Don't talk about your father that way," Mom says, scolding me, despite their ugly divorce. A mischievous smile crosses her face. "Though Dirk sure is a nice slab, isn't he?" She giggles, and I join in.

I'm staring into Dirk Dog's eyes as he starts to introduce the show when I feel the weed start to really hit. I let his dulcet tones wash over me as I slouch further into my seat.

"Welcome to *Myths of the Forgotten Sanctuary*. I'm Dirk Dog, and I sure hope you're ready to find some stone shrines, pray to the great volcano, and win some a-MAZE-ing prizes!"

Ah good, they went with a Japanese appropriated—sorry, "inspired"—theme this time. I'm only half-Japanese, but looking past Dirk and seeing the amount of gongs, Sakura trees, giant plastic sushi and sashimi, and...bamboo and pandas? Good to see they know their Asian culture.

I'm already unimpressed, and this thing has just started. I feel myself sliding lower and lower until the top of my head is tucked under the curve of the seat. Heading deep into what I call my "inevitable weed slouch", I keep my eyes on Dirk, and that's when I see him start to change.

For just the barest of seconds, his eyes flash a fiery red, and I swear I see fangs, dripping with venom as he speaks.

The world around me starts to warble in and out. Sounds muffle, my mind wanders. Jesus, I had only taken one or two hits. I shouldn't be feeling like this. The only time I ever got this high this fast was when—

Oh no.

I scramble into my bag and take a good hard look at its contents. I can just make out the words scribbled on the side of the pen-shaped cartridge. It should say *Calm Your Tits*, my favorite anxiety reducing strain, but instead, emblazoned in red, are the words *Sea Weed*—my go-to, all-encompassing strain for when I really want to feel it.

I wonder when the hell I swapped them out and curse myself for making such a dumb move.

"On today's show, these three pairs are going to work their way through a Japanese legend, hoping to find the Golden Chopsticks hidden in the maze, so they can pick the lock and get their prize at the end of the Sanctuary. Today's prize is...an all-expense paid cruise to the coasts of Jamaica!"

Mom slaps my knee when she sees that I'm still slouched, holding my pen in my hands. The strike jolts me from my thoughts and sends my pen rattling to the ground.

"Dammit, Martha," Mom says, hissing through her teeth. She bends down to try and grab my vape.

Dirk's voice starts to warble more noticeably, and I panic, wondering how I'm going to make it through this taping with the paranoia and giggles starting to set in.

"Say it with me folks," Dirk says, getting ready to start the chant that begins the show. "*Infernum resurget!*"

Wait... That's not the show's catchphrase.

The crowd booms back.

"*Infernum resurget!*"

And, just as the Latin phrase commanded, Hell rises from the floor in a burst of flame.

"What the fuck?" I yell, as the world catches fire around me. From my low position in my seat, I see a fire—somehow sharp and burning all at once—strike the audience around me and my mom, like a swirling scythe cutting down human crop.

"Stay down!" I shout, catching Mom's eyes from my slumped position. Thank god she's still bent over, one hand on my vape pen. A spray of blood catches her surprised face, and I feel the shower of liquid rain on my face, my eyes stinging from the intrusion.

Mom screams. I'm trying to recover my vision from the blood, and I'm grateful she still seems unharmed.

"Martha, what's happening?"

I have no answer as the fire rages overhead, burning a path through the crowd, until it stops as quickly as it came. There is stillness around us, but beyond is the crackling of burning flesh and soft drips of blood falling from chairs.

"You can sit up now," Dirk's voice singsongs from the stage.

My mom meets my eyes, and I nod, reassuring her slowly. I worm my way back up the seat while Mom resumes her sitting position.

"Oh god," she moans. It's all I can do to stop from vomiting, looking at the bloodied, burned mess of the audience around us.

"Not quite," Dirk says, giggling. "Though you all certainly treat this buffoon like one." He gestures toward his body with a look of disgust. "Anyways, back to the program, yeah?"

It's then that I notice the three pairs of contestants are still standing next to him. The rest of the studio, however, is empty. No crew. No viewers.

Just the eight of us, Dirk Dog, and piles of flesh, bones, and ash.

Dirk raises his hand to his eyes, shielding them from the overhead lights, his irises flashing red.

This time, I know it's not the weed haze.

"Just the two of you out there, then? Got quite lucky there. I love a good happenstance," he says. "Alright, come on down and join the fun."

I don't know why I say it and I can only blame the weed, but it pops out. "There's only supposed to be three teams."

Dirk grins, a devilish, wicked thing. "Ah, you're right." He snaps his fingers, a crisp sound that reverberates throughout the empty studio.

And just like that, the three pairs standing next to him quickly turn to two as a suburban-looking wife and husband turn to a pile of dust in front of our eyes.

"This is happening, right?" Mom asks next to me, sounding like the stoned one between us.

"I... I think it really is."

Dirk beckons us forth. "Now, now, problem solved. Time to play, Martha."

My heartbeat jams for a moment when I hear my name, wondering how he knew it.

Nowhere to go but to the stage, so we amble through the staggered seats and what once was our fellow audience members. Mom slips for a second on a flap of skin on the ground, and I catch her before she falls.

"See? A great team already," Dirk comments.

On the stage, I wave to the other contestants. A brother and sister team, both delivery drivers from the South, and a gay couple from Silicon Valley donning matching rainbow-framed glasses.

Dirk claps, delighted at our introductions. "Okay, let's do this," he says. "I'm not even going to bother telling you my real name because I'm fairly certain your tongues can't pronounce it, so you can just keep calling me 'Dirk'.

"I want to play a game with you all. That's what you're here for, right? It'll be just like *Myths of the Forgotten Sanctuary*, but a little jazzed up. Trying to entice the audience back home, after all." He points to the ground. "We love your show down there, and I'm trying to get a promotion, so I thought I'd show them a little...Earthbound magic. See just how far you're willing to go to live. That's part of the prize. A wonderful cruise and your life. Only room for two though."

Dirk leads us to three plastic-walled containers, just big enough to fit us inside. Across from them, a set of chairs with far too many electrical wires sticking out of them.

"Round one," he says. "Trivia and a skills test. A bit of a culinary game, if you will."

He snaps his fingers and I'm somehow inside the plastic container, looking out at my mother rigged to the chair on the other side.

Dirk faces the three of us in the containers. "Tonight, you're making sushi. And the first two to complete their ball of rice, top it with some fresh goodies, and eat it, move along to the next round. And you three,"—he points at Mom and the others in the chair—"are doing some good ol' fashioned trivia. With an extra buzz of course." He pauses for dramatic effect, and I swear I can hear my competitors' hearts pounding. "Go!"

He snaps his fingers again, and all hell breaks loose.

The plastic container fills with insects. Bees, flying around my head. Spiders, grubs as fat as my thumb, scorpions on the ground, stabbing their tails, searching for something to murder. Beneath their wriggling bodies and spindly legs, hundreds of grains of rice. A tiny plate on a ledge rests at my waist.

Next to me, I hear one of the boys from Silicon Valley shrieking in pain. "I'm allergic!" he yells, though I know Dirk doesn't care. "I'm fucking allergic to bees! Ow, goddammit!" I can only imagine he's been stung.

I have to stay calm. Gotta focus and get out of here. Win for me and Mom. I can hear her, through the chaos and the weed haze, yelling words in response to Dirk's trivia questions, yelping now and then after a horrible electrical whirring.

I reach into my purse, grab my pen, and huff, deep and long. That marijuana hits my lungs, and my nerves calm despite the chaos in my container. Bending over, I start to grab grains of rice between my fingers, stacking them into a small mound of rice. I ignore the hardness of the spider legs dancing across my hands, and the crunchy exoskeletons of scorpions resting against my flesh as I reach for rice over and over until I can't see anymore and my rice is some kind of sushi size.

Not done yet though, remembering Dirk's directions. I grab a grub, thick and slimy between my fingers and place it on top of the rice like a piece of sashimi. God, can't slam it back as much as I want to. Heart is racing, throat is tightening. I snag another hit from my vape, trying to get myself to relax—*Jesus Christ, this Sea Weed hits fast*—and my vision is dancing.

I grab the rice with the grub wiggling on top, open my mouth, toss it back. Don't think about the wetness, the bitterness, the bees swarming around me.

Just eat.

With the "sushi" swallowed, I turn to Dirk and show him my tongue. A bee takes that as an invitation to sting my exposed muscle.

"Beezus Christ!" I shout, flicking the bastard away, feeling an itch already crawling across my mouth. I take another hit of Sea Weed to dull the pain. Dirk smirks, snaps his fingers, releases me from the plastic prison.

"Well done, Martha." The restraints on Mom's arms fall to the ground, and she stands and hugs me, wobbly on her feet.

"Trivia never was my strong suit," she says into my neck. I can smell the burned edges of her hair from the electric shocks. My mom gasps, looking over my shoulder. "Honey, don't look."

I look. The boy from Silicon Valley is crumpled at the bottom of the container, swollen from bee stings. Spiders and scorpions are making homes of his flesh.

His partner, still hooked to the electric chair is sobbing. My heart breaks.

"No, no, Derek!" he cries.

Dirk makes feigns a pained expression, sucks air through his teeth. "Oh, no. I'm sorry, that's the incorrect answer. I was looking for 'Karl Marx'." He hits a button, and a crackling fills the air as the boy strapped in the chair writhes in pain. The electricity doesn't relent, and the smell of burning flesh and singed hair fills the air in waves.

My mom's skin turns gray as he dies. Her hand shoots to my purse, rifling within. "Gimme that blunt."

"Mom, it's not a blunt. You can't just call everything that."

"Whatever. Your pen."

"It's not in there." I reach into my pocket, where I placed the vape in a hurry, and hand it to her. "You're just going to want to—"

Mom hits the pen, sucking a lungful of Sea Weed into her system. Okay, then.

Her shoulders relax as she releases the vapor into the open air. "Oh, shit, that's good," she says through a slight wheeze and a cough. I fight back a weed-induced giggle, realizing this is the first time my mom and I are getting high together.

The room fills with more sobbing as the brother and sister pair are released from their devices, having completed the task. The sister is covered in spiders and she pulls a bee from her eye with a shaking hand. What should be the white of her eye was firetruck red already.

Dirk claps, enamored with the outcome. "Wonderful work! Alright, we're going to do something a little unprecedented and just move right to round three: the maze. I can feel my friends downstairs getting a little restless. So, what do you say... Would you like to hear the legend?"

Before anyone can respond, the woman from the other team rushes at Dirk, her shoulder lowered for a tackle. She's an inch away, yelling a string of curses at Dirk when he snaps his fingers. In the blink of an eye, she's gone, and in her place, a gong with a diameter four feet across appears. Dirk, a mallet in his hand, looks at the brother, his eyes wide with panic at his sister's untimely transformation.

"So sorry," Dirk says, not a hint of regret in his voice. He shakes the mallet in his direction. "But that's against the rules. You've been eliminated." He raises his arm, ignoring the brother, pleading with Dirk to stop. The mallet strikes the sister-gong, and the sound that rings out is loud and sharp and painful, the effects of the marijuana warbling the vibrations in and out.

Dirk strikes it again, and then a third time. Upon the final strike, the brother, his arm outstretched toward Dirk, explodes into thousands of pieces of flesh and bones, all of which strike me and Mom.

Dirk winces. "Oooh, always did love a good sliming. Like those 90s kid's game shows." He laughs. "Okay, so back to round three." I can barely hear him, my ears wrecked from the horrid sound of the gong. Mom looks disoriented too, blood and flesh stuck to her face.

"As you know, this game ends with you successfully—or not—navigating a maze in the sanctuary to find the key based on a legend I tell you." Mom and I glance at the temple-like structure, looking at the rooms that are growing by the dozen before our eyes. "Upping the ante. No child's play here," he says.

He hands us two scrolls, then reads from his own. It's a map of sorts, and I try to memorize the path to the goal: a pair of Golden Chopsticks in a hub at the center. "Now pay attention." His voice is stern and my eyes flick back to him. "1100 AD, nearing the end of Heian period Japan, a girl is lost on the seaside. She can hear her mother calling her name, but can't see her through the thick fog. Her eyes drop to the sand, spotting bird footprints in the wet grains. She follows them, hears her mother's voice getting louder. The prints disappear and the girl hears a flapping of wings overhead. They pass each other in the fog, voices growing distant again. She reaches the other side, has grown forty years older. Her mom exits, and dies, ten years past her life expectancy." He stops.

"Is that it?" I ask.

"What the hell does that have to do with anything?" Mom asks, annoyed.

Dirk laughs that same devilish laugh. "Nothing. Some stupid legend I made up on the fly to distract you from the time already ticking down." He points to a clock counting down from fifteen minutes. Thirty seconds have passed. "Better get going."

He snaps his fingers and he's at the top of a tall lifeguard's chair, a megaphone in hand.

"God DAMMIT," Mom yells, and the two of us book it to the maze.

The dangers of the maze are fast made apparent as I almost walk off a ledge I didn't see coming. Mom grabs the back of my shirt, saving me from the spikes below.

"We have to be slow," she says. "Meticulous." She takes a long drag off my vape. I grab it from her and do the same, hoping the weed will help us focus in and drown out the fear. I hear Dirk, narrating our every move.

The timer clicks down, every second like a cannon blast in my ears. With the weed flowing through our veins, we calmly wade through a pit of snakes, following the map across a rickety bridge over a pit of acid.

Dirk snaps his fingers into the megaphone. Shit.

Even more Hell comes knocking at our heels. The set begins to catch fire beneath us, flames so close I can feel my skin throbbing in protest. "Mom, go!" I yell, trying to push her up the ladder we're climbing. Thorns sprout from the rungs, penetrating our palms. The ladder feels endless, but according to the map, the Golden Chopsticks should be in the room at the end.

Mom yelps in pain. I grab the beanie from atop my head and hand it to her so she can cushion her hands. I laugh, thinking how my "lesbian clothing", as Mom called it, is the only thing saving her hide.

She climbs faster and I'm thankful she moves so well for a woman of sixty-five because the flames have started to lick my heels and I can feel blisters forming.

We tumble into the room where the Golden Chopsticks are hovering, by some hellish magic. Mom tries to grab them, but her hand hits an invisible wall snapping one of her fingers backward.

She lets out a string of curse words I didn't know she knew. "What the hell are we supposed to do?"

I remember the legend he told us was meaningless but figured maybe there was something there after all. "Together?" I scream over the roaring fire. Mom nods and we reach out toward the chopsticks, bringing Mom and daughter together. Our fingers curl around the golden wood.

The world spins and turns black.

A loud SNAP resounds in my skull.

I feel gravel on my palms, feel sun on my skin and open my eyes. My mom is next to me, on her hands and knees. She's a little worse for the wear, huffing and puffing, cradling her hand. Hurt, but alive.

Can't say the same about the building. Before us, the TV studio is alight with flames.

On the ground next to us, a pair of Golden Chopsticks and an envelope. Mom opens it, finding two pairs of cruise tickets inside.

I guess...we won.

There's a part of me that will probably never process what just happened. A little piece I'll tuck away inside. Mom will do the same.

Trauma response later. Right now, I just want to sit here with my mom, who I am very grateful is still alive, ready to annoy me another day. I reach for my purse, somehow still hooked over my shoulder. Without speaking, I take one last hit of my pen and pass it to Mom.

She inhales like a pro.

Stoned as shit, but alive and mostly well, we sit watching the studio burn, wondering how we were going to explain what happened when the sirens we hear in the distance finally arrive.

Chapter 3
Now I Am Just the Thing That Cooks

People love to say, "Rome wasn't built in a day," but I'm here to tell you that it damn well could have been if I'd been at the helm.

I haven't exactly built a city, but I have conceived of a way to build one, with the helping hands of legions across multiple periods of history, places—hell, even dimensions, all at once. You see that chrome machine, under the fluorescent lightning in the middle of the room?

That's mine. The Multi-Tooled. Trademarked. A multitool that contains multitudes. That's what it is. On the nose, fine, but does it matter when it's a very nice nose to be on the tip of? My machine can do it all. Open portals, send through a part of yourself to occupy space on the other side, all while able to maintain your presence somewhere else. I'm hoping I can bring things back, too. Move things through dimensions with the ease of a shiny machine.

My kid, she's been getting to this age where the ugly in this world starts to show itself to her. Twelve years old and she's becoming aware of how messed up things can be. Her big hang-up these days is agonizing over world hunger. I imagine her anxiety would worsen if she knew just how bad poverty and food disparities were in other dimensions, too.

The machine hasn't made the jump yet—with human flesh, at least—to other domains. But I've seen into them in an attempt to connect with the spaces that exist elsewhere. I've seen creatures that could never breathe here on Earth starving just as much as anyone here. Entire civilizations in turmoil when whatever passes as sustenance disappears.

So, here's the plan. I'm going to dimensions that have more food than they know what to do with. I'm going to take the surplus, and do nothing but prepare food for the places that need it most. Just want my daughter to be proud.

My partner has told me on more than one occasion just how much this won't work. In fact, she's over in the corner now running diagnostics—and her mouth.

"This Robin Hood bullshit isn't going to work, Carla," Darcy says, her pencil scribbling measurements of distance to the Sorfin Domain.

"Darcy, please," I say. "Melia wants this, we've got the machine to make it happen. We can make a difference." I almost hate how much I sound like a walking platitude.

"The only thing we're making is a mistake. Do you even know how to cook?"

"That's the thing about the Multi-Tooled. With the MT, I can send portions of myself out to multiple places at once and bring them back with all the skills I could never dream of accruing in a lifetime."

"So, you learn to cook."

"Yes, and also learn the logistics of how to streamline the process to bring meals to the places that need them the most."

Darcy lets out a gust of wind that sounds somewhere between disapproval, disbelief, and annoyance. A no-good soup of negativity.

She doesn't get it, but I appreciate her agreeing to help me all the same.

"Tomorrow, I think," I say to Darcy. "Tomorrow, I'm ready to try to make the jump."

Another sigh from my partner. "Fine, things do look like they're ready. Won't be more ready, most likely."

"That last rat we put through came back just fine," I say, nodding my head toward Reggie in her cage. She had a mountain of cheese that she had snagged from the other dimension. Had placed them all in her little rat-sized pouch and carried them through the other side like she'd been trained to do it her whole life.

"Yep, and no extra legs or missing eyes. Just some added poundage from all that cheese she has now."

I walk over to Darcy, place my arms around her and hold her tight. "It'll be fine. But just in case..." I say, whispering into her ear.

Darcy cranes her neck and kisses me on the lips. "Better get one more good shag in before you come back with an abundance of lady parts or something."

I quirk my eyebrows. "Wouldn't that make things better?"

She grins. "For you, at least. For me, it would make this whole relationship more trouble than it's worth."

She gets a smack for that one.

I sneak one last glance at the MT, gleaming in the corner, looking ready for action.

"Tomorrow."

***

It's tomorrow, and I must admit I'm a little nervous.

The day feels perfect enough. Shining sun, few clouds to cut through the pounding heat. Darcy's hand gripped in mine on the right, Melia's much smaller fingers curled into my left hand. My girls, my world.

Darcy has her eyes fixed on the MT, almost staring it down and daring it to fuck me up. Like she's willing images of crushed metal and broken wires into its circuits so it knows she means business.

Melia though, her eyes are on me. Those big brown eyes, wide and adoring.

I'm taking them all in, wondering what it would be like to see into both their worlds at once, because soon, that's what I'll be doing when I'm hooked up to the MT.

"Today," I say, wondering if we'll walk out the same way we came in.

"Today," Darcy says, her forehead resting against mine, a shiver in her voice.

"Today," Melia says, giving my hand a little squeeze.

The three of us take our places in the lab. Melia, behind safety glass, parked thirty yards from the MT just in case. Darcy, over at the console so she can monitor my vitals and the Multi-Tooled's signals. It's up to her to get me hooked in from place to place.

I step into the confines of the machine. Her claws wrap around my wrists, locking them in. My feet, bound as well, tingle at the cold of metal.

Once secure, the machine whirrs to life, and it takes my body from a vertical to a horizontal position.

There are no more words. Just concentration. We expended all our worries on the way over. All the what ifs and promises.

The machine begins to slide my body into its center, circular, long like an MRI. I enter its mouth.

My world becomes a series of beeps, spinning and vibrating, the screams of a machine working its magic. I try and close out the crushing noise, try to fill my veins with hope and positivity. Don't let bad thoughts in.

My arms rotate outwards in the machine, gently placing them into smaller tunnels at the sides. I think about how I look like I'm doing my best impersonation of Jesus, and I hope I don't die in this machine.

I think I must have been inside this death trap, cycling through its motions for what feels like hours. It sounds like a jet revving its engines in my ears, like someone trapped a hurricane in here with me. My eyes are watering, I feel spittle at the corner of my mouth, and everything is coming in and out of focus as darkness descends.

And that's when I see it.

Our kitchen at home. The tiny blue toaster, the black fridge. Melia's straight-A report card hung by magnets. And I don't just see it... I'm there. I feel it. Feel the bottoms of my bare feet on the linoleum.

The world becomes calmer. I'm home, even though I can still feel the MT whirring like there's no tomorrow. I'm settling into myself in my kitchen, trying to calm my breathing. I reach out, grab the cold metal of the fridge handle, and get to work.

It takes some time as I find my bearings. I should be able to make a sandwich in three minutes, but so far this PB & J is kicking my ass and clocking in at what feels like fifteen. Everything moves slower, like trying to swim through thick syrup on a muggy day with concrete tied to your ankles.

Finally, I do it. The other slice of bread on the other side, making the sandwich a sandwich. I open my mouth, work my tongue even as I feel spit flying from it, from the mouth of the me in the chamber of the MT.

"Back!" I shout.

I hope Darcy can hear me on the other side.

I'm standing in my kitchen, ten miles from the lab. I'm in the MT's mouth, ten miles from my home.

And then, I'm nowhere.

***

My eyes flutter open. Everything feels stuck together. As I blink, releasing my eyelids from their crusty partnerships, I inventory my body parts. Two of each on the leg and arm front. A good number of toes and fingers. A face that feels less numb with each passing moment.

I'm on my back still and feel the cold arms of the MT around me. A pressure on my abdomen.

My eyesight is blurry, but I make out the vague form of a circle on my stomach. A plate, from my kitchen.

I turn my head to the right, finding Darcy's eyes. They're worried—understandable when your wife has just crossed through space and time and made a sandwich in your kitchen while lying in a lab, and then brought said sandwich back with her.

A sandwich, which I can see, is held in Melia's hands, to my left. I beckon to her, unable to find words quite yet, and she passes the PB & J to me.

"No, don't," Darcy says.

But it's too late. I bring the morsel to my lips, and take a bite.

I chew, thoughtful, enjoying the crunch of the peanut butter and the refined sugar in the jelly. The bread is soft. I swallow.

My dry lips crack a smile as I find my voice. "Chef's kiss." I grin.

Darcy let's out a deep breath. Plants a big smackeroo on my lips. "Chef's kiss," she whispers to me.

***

I'm in the machine at least fourteen hours a day. At this point, the Multi-Tooled has become another part of me. That first time, we started small. Someplace familiar with a task I already knew how to do.

Now, we had to test the limits.

I spend as much time as I can brokering deals with other planets in a variety of dimensions. Talking with world leaders here on Earth. What I was hoping to do was see how far it could take me and what I could learn. How to cook in other worlds. The best way to prepare delicacies that hungry mouths could enjoy. I needed to know my own limits just as much as the MT's.

What I found is that I could be in at least three places at once—four if you counted the inside of the machine. I could walk around, carry conversations, work my brain and learn new skills. Take notes on the flora and fauna of each destination and how to optimize their nutritional intake. I could do all of this while I did the same thing somewhere else.

And when I came back, which was getting easier and easier each trip, I could bring things with me. Knowledge, items, food. Hope.

It went on like this for weeks.

I pushed myself to be able to occupy a fifth space, upping my productivity.

A long day had passed while I spent time in the Sorfin, learning the logistics of their finfala plant trade. I'm still thinking about their beautiful pink hills in the shower when I notice it.

A mole? Or skintag? I don't know, but it's occupying the space on my stomach between my navel and my right breast. And it's a bright blue, the color of the sea. I couldn't help but think it looked like a grain of the very finfala I'd spent all day learning to grow in Sorfin.

I pluck it off, a thin line of blood spilling from my skin.

I don't tell Darcy. It heals.

I grow another.

It goes on like this for another few days. I'm climbing out of the MT after fifteen hours in its clutches. I had a meeting off-planet to discuss mass production of the machine, where patents were less necessary. The donors and I decided to get this going on a larger scale. The only thing better than a dozen mes (almost up to fifteen placements at once!) was a hundred of these machines. A thousand of these things.

It was amazing to see the solution of so many problems universe-wide in this chrome goddess standing before me.

I think about the blue growths that have multiplied over the terrain of my skin. I feel another, fuzzier than usual between my shoulder blades. Darcy still hasn't seen these undesirable things I've brought back from my travels. Souvenirs that no one would want. The first time in my life I've been thankful to be too tired to sleep together. I don't think she's seen my naked body in a month.

Pulling my legs over the side of the MT's gurney, something fleshy catches my eye. My heart stutters when I see it's a green sprout shooting from my wrist. I pull my shirt down over the skin, hoping Darcy doesn't see it. I'll deal with it later.

I always do.

***

It happened so slowly at first, but then, all at once.

That sounds like such a cliché and it makes me happy to at least resemble something human.

The sprout on my wrist? The green thing? Turns out it was arugula. I found out by tearing a sprig off my wrist and eating myself.

The arugula grows across my body like a rash. Or acne. It now fields at least half my arm, up to my elbow, and the blue speckles of finfala have become unquantifiable. Everywhere.

The parts of me that I can see look like a Christmas tree. I don't entirely know what's happening. Perhaps I'm taking back more than I can chew from each dimension, each space I've sent myself. Echoes of my journeys left on my permanent body like scars of the good deeds I'm doing.

I should be scared, but I can't get myself to feel anything but the urge to enter the MT and continue learning and growing and feeding the mouths of the hungry everywhere I can as fast as possible.

Darcy finally sees it when I return from Planet Taluga with the mushy, rotted skin of the flora they consume filling the length of my cheek.

She screams.

Curses.

Cries.

"CCarla, CCarla," she weeps, observing the green and blue farm that is my body beneath my clothes. "How could you fucking do this?"

She pleads with me to never go in that machine again.

I tell her it's my destiny. We—me and the MT—we have a job to do. We are going to help so, so many people.

She says something about Melia never seeing me again. I tell her that Melia understands, and together we'll make this work.

Darcy grabs clumps of my arugula and pulls it from my skin, uprooting the green gift the MT has given us.

With one hand, I push her. She falls. Hits her head. All I can do is think about how the red of her blood looks like the nutrient-rich lake on Sorfin that I've figured out how to disperse to other dimensions to give strength to their fauna.

I call emergency services for my wife. Hope she hasn't expired. Expired, food on shelves, so wasteful so, meaningless...

Pushing my swirling thoughts to the side, I run. Take the car back to the lab, take Melia with me. She's petrified, I think, but I was right.

She understands.

We go in silence. Reach the lab.

I teach her how to work the console. I tell her where I want to go.

She nods. Gives me a hug and tells me she loves me and is so proud that her mommy is healing the world.

The MT calls to me with that hum I have grown to adore so much. "Carla," it says, whirring a tornado of gratitude and faith in my abilities. "Carla."

It tells me to climb into its womb once more.

I abide.

The machine takes hold of me. Crucifies me again and I know this will be where I spend my existence.

I enter twenty dimensions, twenty planets, twenty kitchens and offices of government leaders. Twenty labs where I have been building more of these machines.

Don't exit. Don't *want* to exit.

My body on Earth, in the lab with Melia, has reached its natural limit.

I feel myself bringing things back to myself that I don't intend to. An arm of a Sorfin farmer. A leg from a politician. Food, liquid, more food, and so much liquid becomes a part of me. I can feel the limits of my flesh tested inside the grasp of the MT. I feel bulbous, swollen, full with the glut of other worlds.

Another me returns to the same pocket of space-time that Melia is in. I walk around the lab, a shadow of myself, and hold her tight as she cries, seeing what her mother has become.

Averting her eyes, I tell her I love her and that her work is done. That Mommy will be feeding the universe, one mouth at the time. I send her back home to where I hope she still has her other mom. We were Carla and Darcy. Darla. Darla, Darla, my little Starla. Stars, just like all the planets. All the places I'm becoming. All the things I've already become.

Melia scurries off, a tearful goodbye. I walk to myself and the MT. I see myself and my new, evolving body.

It's a monstrous, drooling, lumpy, smelly mass of what was once a human Me, consumed by the whirring of the machine. My body is a multitude of things from every dimension I've been. A swirl of body parts and flesh, remnants of all the mes who have escaped to other worlds.

It's ugly. It's beautiful.

I know what I am now.

I was a hopeful scientist. I wanted to do what I could to make my little girl proud and change the universe for the better.

I'm doing those things, but the me that's here. The me on this slab inside the MT...

Well, now I am just the thing that cooks.

I retreat back into myself, feel myself become another head on that flesh pile inside the MT in my original world. Can't communicate with the other mes anymore. They're independent from the original me, working away on our shared mission, and I hope they are making good progress.

Thinking is hard.

Cooking is easy. Growing is easy.

Easy.

Easy.

Chapter 4
When the Pests Come Marching In

T he crops sing under the blood-red moon.

Stalks of wheat and corn, vines of tomato, root vegetables, and lush orchards, all pray to the red and black sky.

Mother Tera can only smile at the bounty she knows will be harvested tonight. Her long, silky black robes puddle at her feet. Not the most conventional attire for late night farming, but ceremony is ceremony and Mother Tera promised the best to her clients.

She glides down the row of apple trees, pulls a bright red fruit from the sturdy, healthy limbs. The skin shines under the light of the moon like the treasure that it is. Mother Tera bites down, a loud crunch resounding throughout the empty fields.

Inside the apple, the flesh is tinged with red.

Perfect, Tera thinks. She licks the juice from the corners of her mouth, savoring the taste of iron on her tongue.

The apple—and the rest of the produce on the farm—is a thing of great wonder. An impeccable celebration of farm-grown food, specialized just for vampires...and any other creature who might enjoy blood-infused meals.

Tera had been toiling away at the logistics of pulling off such a feat for centuries. Granted, at over a twelve-hundred years old, she's had plenty of time to devote to her craft.

When the existence of monsters surprised the world, it didn't take long for their pleasures to be monetized. To become a prize of the entertainment industry. Reality television (Tera really needed to catch up on *Transylvania Shore*) and cooking competition shows (Tera had made a guest appearance on *Ghoul's Kitchen* just last month) had taken over the airwaves. Tera thought it to be hilarious how humans found so much joy in the very creatures who rejoice in their blood.

The community considered Mother Tera to be a savior in more than one right: a resource provider for the monster community, and a herald of safety for humans. Her farm marked a turn to slow the flow of victims that was dwindling the living population. And the blood-minded creatures of the world were over the moon at what her produce provided.

Monster chefs all over the globe craved what she had to offer. Her fruits, vegetables, and grains had become an overnight sensation when chefs realized they could, at last, eat and make *real* food again. Elaborate dishes that could satisfy the need for fresh blood and death would earn them Michelin stars, without the bloodshed. Ethically-sourced ingredients that appeased the blood cravings, provided nutrition, and did so in a way politicians could approve of.

A miracle, in short.

Mother Tera taps the earth beneath her feet.

A miracle, sure. But also, a little, teensy bit of fabrication. *If they only knew...* Tera thinks, noticing the almost imperceptible sound of metal reinforcing the ground—and the ceiling— deep under the soil.

She reminds herself to check the under-fields later tonight. After the harvest.

The blood-red moon catches the twinkle in her eyes. Six hours before the sun. Six hours to harvest the hundreds of acres of cultivated land. Six hours to do it all, while beating back the inevitable pests that come with the territory of running a multi-million dollar business that caters to monsters.

Once word had gotten out that Mother Tera was revitalizing the culinary world, thieves made it their mission to get a piece of her product. They tracked her harvest to the lunar eclipse, and they came in droves.

Thankfully, Mother Tera knows a thing or two about defending her crop. Another perk of being as old as the dirt beneath her feet was that her strength had grown over the centuries, aided by the added nutritional boosts of her food.

Tera bites into the apple again, feeling the substance bolster her muscles. She was one vampire who never—ever—went hungry.

The moon rises to its full potential. The night grows a deeper red. *Time to begin.*

Tera summons her brethren, her bats and rats, all a part of her vampiric animal coven. Her mind calls out orders to those who can hear, to those who will obey and be rewarded handsomely by the end of the night. A feast for all, to celebrate a successful harvest.

A cloud of black wings and the rumble of the beating of thousands of feet breaks across the chill night air. A stampede of rats and fleets of bats awaits further instruction.

Mother Tera flies to the middle of the fields, the dead center of the vast acreage of her farm. The cold air causes her robes to ribbon behind her, like a magnificent eel cutting through the sky.

Her fangs descend from her blood-red gums as she revels in power.

Hovering above the crops, Mother Tera conducts her orchestra of the harvest. Her arms swirl, her mind pushes commands to her army. One by one, the animals clip the produce from its stems, unearth vegetables from the clumped soil, and carry the bounty to the appropriate bins to be packaged and shipped to customers around the globe in the morning.

It just has to be protected until then.

With the animals in motion, Mother Tera opens her ears to the sounds of the night. She's comforted by the noise of fluttering wings and tiny feet on the dirt, but her ears prickle with a noise she both dreads and desires. She may be old, but she's got a lot of fight in her ancient bones.

Human feet. Heavy boots.

Uninvited guests.

Mother Tera grins a vicious smile and flies in the direction of the footsteps. She hears heartbeats, indicating the undead haven't arrived...

Yet.

Tera soars toward the gaggle of humans, back-to-back with guns held tight in their sweaty palms. She *tsk tsks*, her tongue snapping against her pointed teeth. They should know better than to try and steal from her.

The time for mercy has long passed.

She is soundless and lands on top of one of the men, her teeth flashing in the night before sinking into his throat. The reinforced leather of his collar is no match for the strength of her bite, and her teeth rips the flesh from his throat. Even though she has feasted on her produce for years, the taste of the real thing, mingled with flesh, still excites her. She swallows her mouthful, neck flap and all, a ring of red around her lips. He dies in a gurgling puddle.

The other thieves turn their guns toward Tera, shout obscenities in her face before pulling the trigger. Her skin sizzles as the holy water soaked bullets graze her arms and neck, but lucky for her they're terrible shots. Or, maybe, she's just *that* fast.

Gnarled claws lengthen from the tips of her fingers as a snarl paints it way across her face. The slashing begins, and soon the robbers are in pieces on the ground, their blood watering the soil beneath them. Tera doesn't stop to bask in their blood—she can already hear more unwanted guests. She struggles to discern the sound of the wind fluttering against leather above her head, but she makes it out just in time to dart out of reach of the flying vampires hellbent on stealing her crop and her life in the process.

She makes short work of them—they're newly turned and inexperienced. Mother Tera doesn't hesitate as she ends their existence. She knows no sympathy for her own kind when they seek to take from her.

Tera catches each of the nascent vampires mid-air and throws them toward the apple orchard, impaling them on tree limbs. She hears the sound of flesh exploding into wet dust, bone shards shooting in every direction.

Such a shame we're so much work to clean up, Tera thinks. *No added nutrients to the crop, either. A waste.*

Tera sighs, pushing air through her dead lungs in exasperation. Less than an hour in, and already the fields are wet with blood and covered in vampire refuse. The rats and bats are still hard at work harvesting the crop, and Tera feels a sense of pride welling in her chest. For creatures who garner so much disdain, they're her most dedicated farmhands.

Silence again, save for the sounds of her animal coven gathering crops. Tera faces the moon, closes her eyes and feels its energy caressing her cheeks. The soft earth hums beneath her feet, absorbing the blood offerings to the soil. *Some last-minute fertilization never hurts*, Tera supposes.

She senses more bodies approaching, readies herself for a fight.

And the pests come marching in.

For hours, she beats flesh, rips throats out of human robbers. She explodes her vampire brethren in a parade of blood and bone. She cackles into the sky, her skin glistening under the blood moon as the night witnesses her handiwork. Mother Tera is covered from head to toe in viscera, shining the deepest red under the scarlet light.

Even by her standards, the sea of scourge felt never ending. She'd long pushed herself past what she thought were her limits.

With every head she smashes, she imagines the dishes showcased in the culinary world using her produce. Pastas covered in red sauce from her tomatoes. Fruit pies baked with her blood-infused fruit. Tacos in scarlet corn tortillas, and cakes topped with her bloody almond crumble.

Another death, another dish.

Mother Tera is happy to kill for her legacy.

By the end of the night, she's lost count of how many insects she's crushed. This year, there were more than ever, but as the last tree is plucked of apples, relief floods her chest. No matter what came for her crops, she had the perfect pesticide running through her veins.

Greed is quite the fuel for the fire, it seems.

The first rays of sun creep over the horizon, and the rodents disappear into the shadows from whence they came, their share of fruit scraps and other treats held in their claws to savor later. Mother Tera sends a wave of gratitude to her animal coven. They've earned their keep tonight, just as they will again next harvest. The fleet of trucks packed with her produce rumble to life, on the first legs of their journeys to her customers. It's out of her hands now.

Tera heads inside to her farmhouse, her black silky robes covered in gore. She licks her fingers. All in day's work.

Once inside, Tera heads below ground, down the candlelit steps of her basement where her ears fill with the most glorious noises. The sounds of moans. The cries of help.

Deep underground, she pushes through a set of heavy oak doors and into the vast set of tunnels below her farm. The darkness stretches for miles, underneath every corner of her fields.

She flips a switch, and the room comes to life.

As far as the eye can see, bodies hang from the ceiling, supported by metal gurneys affixed with sets of sturdy chains. Below, medical equipment beeps and whirrs, connected to dangling arms.

Mother Tera takes to the air, flies to the closest body and rubs at the sweat-dotted forehead of the young man lying, still as the dead, on the suspended slab.

He doesn't speak, only moans at Tera's loving stare, boring into his eyes.

"Thank you for your contributions," she whispers to him.

She reaches her hand up and strokes the plant roots that burst through the ceiling, winding down to his chest, anchored into his heart and veins.

Her hand caresses the rubbery, soil-covered root. "Drink up, my sweets."

The roots writhe under her touch, drinking deep from the immobile man, who groans with the renewed suction.

Mother Tera laughs, thinking of all the loss of life the blood moon had witnessed. They couldn't steal a single stalk of corn, let alone foil the *true* heart of her operation, right underneath their feet.

Her secret was safe, and her absolutely one-hundred percent eth-ically-sourced blood-substitute produce was free to be cultivated for another year.

Tera was mother to them all. The thousand living humans, her own personal fertilizer. She took care of them, made sure their roots ran red to the tips of their sprouts. No leaf could be spared when culinary achievements were on the line.

Next year, she'd do it again. Ceremony. Ritual. Harvest. Routine. And when the pests come marching in, she'd defend against them and relish in the showers of their blood.

But for now, she'd thank the tributes, caress each root until every plant knew just how much she loved them all.

Because she did—with every ounce of her unbeating heart—to the moon and back.

Chapter 5
Starfish Pizza Party

The blackest parts of space often hold the most colorful life.

That's one of the things I've learned during my career as a space junker. And it's why I'm out here, heading toward the blackest void in search for something different, something special. I've gotten quite sick of the same gray shards of metal I usually haul.

My ship, known as *The Shed*, crawls forward, the great vacuums in its sides sucking up discarded treasures and debris. I take a bite of pizza, feet propped on the center console of my flight controls. My heart leaps in excitement as the stars come fewer and further between. The blackest part of space. The best part of space.

Another important bit of knowledge? There is no better food combination than crispy yet soft dough, thick, stringy cheese, and crushed and spiced tomato sauce.

My last trip back to Earth, I scored a great deal on a stash of pizzas. Now when I'm hungry, I just need to throw one into the hyperspeed microwave, that I've had installed on *The Shed*. That piece of kitchen machinery has revolutionized space cuisine. Just toss some pre-packaged food onto the conveyor belt there, and it comes out the other side, piping hot and ready for consumption.

Cheese and sauce oozes down my chin, so I brush my long, curly hair away from the food mess. *The Shed* bumbles along through empty space. I'm thankful for the calm ride, as it lets me enjoy my savory meal.

It's taken a while to reach this sector of the black void. Junkers don't usually make it out here in one piece, but for years I've upgraded my ship with the bounties of previous trips so I can meander here for as long as I like.

With another slice of pizza in hand, I head toward the window. My boots feel crazy heavy, as if weighed down by the gravity of the situation. I peer out the window, staring into the inky void around me. It's so dark, almost as if stars themselves are afraid to shine here.

They did, though, once upon a time, shine right here, filling the night with just enough light to see for lightyears. Centuries ago, the stars used to illuminate this corner of space something brilliant. But the war had raged so heavily here that space itself had been wounded, and now the light of the stars is unable to pierce the scar tissue.

"Approaching null space," my onboard artificial intelligence, Charlene, says in her light Southern drawl. (What can I say? I have a soft spot for ranchers.) She continues, "Rhoda, I'm sensing some debris. Shall I open the gate?"

"Do it, darling," I respond.

"You've got it." I hear the mechanical sounds of decompression as the gates unlock, and the vacuum powers on.

I have to be vigilant. The debris out here is known to tear the hulls off spacecrafts of every kind.

But space debris isn't the only concern here. I felt afraid as soon as *The Shed* crossed what felt like some magical threshold guarding this place. Rumor has it that this little corner of null space is haunted. I'm prepared for the danger of space, no matter what form it takes. I'm afraid, but excited, as if I've just slammed a cocktail that sends your head dizzy in drunkenness.

I've spent a lifetime hauling debris from place to place, my ship sucking up and cleaning up after skirmishes and engine failures. I've collected flora and fauna, preserved by the oxygen-free environment. I've netted broken technology and scrap metal, and harvested energy from an abundance of sources.

But I've never caught a ghost.

I can only imagine a trapped soul will fetch a high price on the market. But money aside, the glory smells even sweeter.

The Shed shudders as I dip further into the black. It's an odd shake, though. I'm used to the heavy rumble of machinery, but this time feels different, like the way it might feel to be squeezed rather than shook. I turn on the outside lights, but it's still just darkness.

"There's been an impact," Charlene says, her voice echoing throughout the cabin of the ship.

"Any damage?"

"*The Shed* is intact upon initial scan."

I glance at my watch and make a mental note to check the cameras later to make sure I didn't hit anything. Wouldn't want to get in trouble for a space hit-and-run.

"How's the haul coming?"

"We have reached a wreckage site. The debris on my radar is all around us now. Shall I drop an anchor?"

"Yeah, park her here, darlin'."

The whirring of the vacuum processor starts up, the telltale sign that the ship has found something floating in space and sucked it in. I head to the room where the massive machine looms like an angry giant. The silver container that holds the scrap clanks and thumps as items are pulled into its maw, and I head to the computer to see what's been taken in.

Some kind of flora, the readout suggests. Nothing toxic, according to the safety scan, so it is released to the conveyor belt. The analysis continues as more *thunks* are heard in the container. I feel a trickle of excitement working its way through my chest, and my heart beats faster.

The screen populates the new readout. Fauna. Or at least...*parts* of something animal, something humanoid. The conveyor belt begins spitting those out as well once they're cleared as safe.

I can't wait for the rest of the report, overzealous to see what I've caught.

I make it three steps to the belt before I gag.

The flora is a neon pink fuzz of a plant, and it isn't singular in its biology, like I had assumed. My face scrunches together when I see the plant is a fungus growing out of a fauna, shaping it, and that the humanoid structure—I can't believe my eyes—is a dozen identical legs.

Human legs.

They're churning down the conveyor belt, covered in the pink sponge. They're thighs down to the toes, naked of clothes, just fleshy and pink. No torso, no head, just legs. I cover my mouth and gag again.

At first, I think they're connected, but realize the legs have been ripped from one another, stringy flesh pulled from bone, reminding me of the pizza I've just consumed, the long tendrils of cheese dripping down my face.

In all my years of trawling, I've never seen anything like this.

The container continues to creak and groan under the pressures of the items being sucked onto my ship from the vacuum. I hear more refuse sliding through the metal tubes, the pitch of the whirring changing with each piece it consumes. God, I hope they aren't *all* thighs. I'm a leg girl, for sure, but I prefer them attached to the women I find.

Charlene crackles to life from the speakers. "Did we strike gold, Rhoda?"

"We struck something, alright." I creep closer to the conveyor belt. A sickly-sweet smell permeates the air, reminding me of the cotton candy I used to consume back on Earth with my family. My chest clenches as I think of my dad holding my hand at the carnival. The last I'd heard from him, he called me a space whore, no child of his—a no-good junker, as filthy as the trash I took in.

I was lucky I could escape to space to forget just how mad he was when I came out.

But now, looking at these identical legs—all left legs from what I could tell—covered in this bright, princess-colored pink, I felt a pang of regret that I wasn't back on Earth, with two *attached* feet firm on the ground.

"Charlene, can you double check the scan? This fungus isn't toxic, is it?"

"As far as I can tell, it's stagnant. No spores separating, and no dangerous elements detected."

"And the legs?"

"Quite a bit of them, I reckon," Charlene says, and I laugh at her bluntness.

"Sure is."

"I count twenty-six legs in the container, ten on the belt."

I sigh, unsure how to proceed with this haul. "Well, as long as they aren't alive and kicking."

"Indeed," Charlene says, annoyance in her voice.

Seems a good pun is less impressive to an AI system than I wagered.

After a beat, Charlene speaks again. "I suggest you call the proper authorities regarding the humanoid refuse."

"Good idea."

"I will seal the door behind you."

"You're just full of good ideas. Wouldn't want them to follow, right?"

"Just go, Rhoda." I swear I can here Charlene sigh. Leave it to me to choose an AI that sounds just like my ex.

I head back to command, unnerved by the few dozen left legs covered in pink fungus I was leaving behind me. Maybe the authorities would know what it was.

I sit in my chair, wishing for once that I didn't choose to travel solo. I always enjoyed the solitude—Charlene was all the company I needed anyway—but the haul sitting in my cargo bay... It was already haunting me.

"*The Shed* to Enforcers, *The Shed* to Enforcers," I say over my comms.

Static crackles in my ear. "Enforcers here. Report."

"I've picked up a load from null that I think you might need to look at."

"Report," he says again.

"Well, I've picked up a bundle of humanoid waste. They're legs, I think, covered in pink fuzz."

He's quiet, until his staticky voice asks me to repeat what I've said.

"Legs, sir. Three dozen of them, not attached to anything."

"You said you're in null?"

"I am."

"Get out of there."

"Sir?"

"I said, get out of there. Dump your haul and get the hell—"

The line cuts out, and within a fraction of a second, a long, shrill shrieking emanates from everywhere at once. It's outside the ship, coming through the speakers. It's inside the ship, coming from down the corridor.

The cargo bay!

The screams are unlike anything I've ever heard, like autotuned babies wailing for their mothers through a shroud of cotton.

I race back to the cargo hold, my hands clamped over my ears. I stop, eyes widening as I gaze through the window in the door.

There are legs all over the floor. They've multiplied exponentially.

Through the shrieking, I hear Charlene attempting to reach me. "Rho... Sealing... Don't..." is all I can make out.

I watch in amazement as the legs multiply, from a pile of limbs infected with pink mold to a mass large enough that it almost reaches the door. They aren't just multiplying out of nothing, I notice. Squinting, I focus on a single leg. From the stump of its thigh, a foot forms, just small toes at first, but then the arch and a heel, an ankle, a calf. When the leg splits, the two legs it forms move together at a more acute angle until from the crease between them, a third leg begins to grow.

Over and over, the legs split and grow until they pinwheel, feet pointed in the same direction.

A memory of a tidepool on Earth strikes me, the legs reminding me of a nightmarish version of a starfish regenerating.

As if reading my thoughts, a mouth opens in the center of the leg circle and starts...breathing. It spits out a glob of pink—slimy at first, but drying on the skin—mimicking the consistency of the substance that originally came through the vacuum.

Then comes the screaming. That same eerie wailing that only adds to the cacophony of its brethren's cries. Seconds later, the creature's center begins to pulsate before bursting like a volcano, pink foam shooting in all directions, the legs exploding outwards.

The fallen limbs begin the process all over again.

At this rate, the whole ship will be filled in less than an hour.

I retreat to the kitchen, unsure what the hell to do, but I hope that in here, maybe I can hear Charlene better.

"Char?" I ask, the nerves evident in my voice.

"Yes, Rhoda?"

"What the fuck is going on?"

"It appears we have sucked in a parasitic and regenerative specimen."

"How did the scans miss that?"

"It seems it was activated by the oxygen level in the ship."

"Well, ain't that great."

"It's not."

"I know Char, I know. What should we do?"

"I suggest you open the airlock in the container room. Reverse the vacuum and send it back to space."

I hesitate, wishing we wouldn't have to eject it from the ship. This has got to be an incredible find. "Can we do that?"

"We can. Everything should be bolted down enough. We can replace what isn't."

I wince as I calculate the risk. "Okay, do it."

"Commencing airlock exposure. Commencing purge."

I walk over to my food stash, unpackage a pizza and toss it into the food processor. Eating always calms my nerves, and lord knows I'm buzzing with those right now.

I can still hear the screaming from the distance, can sense the ever-growing pile of limbs, can almost make out the sounds of flesh hitting the metal door, hitting the glass, breaking the—

Oh no, oh no, ohnononono, I repeat in my head, my feet beating against the ground as I race back to the cargo hold only to see a set of legs bursting out the other side of the window.

"Oh, m-my g-god," I stutter.

"Yes?" Charlene responds.

"Now's not the time for jokes, Char," I say, scrambling backwards as the legs—dozens and dozens of legs—spill through the window. They hobble and roll toward me, the neon pink fungus like a flashing warning sign to do everything I can to just get the fuck away from whatever horror is piling up toward me.

The hallway fills with legs, and I backtrack to the kitchen, hearing the ghastly wails of the legs behind me, growing, splitting, growing, splitting, exploding, and doing it all over again all down the corridor.

"Char, open the goddamn airlock! Now!"

"Working on it. Bypassing the system that's trying to keep you from getting sucked out too."

"Faster," I yell through gritted teeth, pulling shut the heavy door to the cafeteria.

I retreat further into the room, away from the door, which is about to explode under the pressure of the legs. I can see bolts loosening, and I pray I'm not about to be drowned in limbs.

Within ten seconds, the door *does* burst inwards, and toes and legs flood the room. I'm knocked to my feet as the ship lurches.

"Processes booted. Opening airlock. Purging."

I crabwalk backward and hear the sounds of oxygen rushing through the ship from the cargo bay. The screaming is deafening, louder than ever. My ears bleed from a combination of the noise and the sudden change in pressure.

Despite the suction, the legs continue to multiply inwards, exploding pink mold everywhere. My skin crawls as the fungus lands on my exposed flesh.

The whooshing air gets louder. The cargo bay must be cleared now, but then I remember the broken window and the busted door.

I almost sob as I start to see the limbs inhaled by the airlock, retreating through the air and back out to space. I imagine the black void sucking them all from my ship as if through a straw.

The suction reaches my body and I hold onto the sturdy food processing machine with as much strength as I have left in me. I hear the sounds of the legs zipping from the room. Loose items follow them—forks, plates, and glass drinkware break against the walls.

My muscles strain, and I know I should be drenched in sweat, but the decompression steals that away, too. Just when I think I might just let go and die, I hear Charlene's voice, almost inaudible over the cacophony caused by the hurricane winds.

"Purge complete."

A split second passes before the suction stops as the airlock slams closed. The ship shudders, almost as if it's trying to catch its breath after vomiting the hundreds of detached legs back into space.

"Cargo bay is clear."

I let out a breath I didn't know I was holding. "Thanks, darlin'," I wheeze. My chest aches.

I came to null space looking for ghosts. The stories were wrong. Null isn't haunted by phantoms, but rather by some strange alien foam that imitates whatever human life it touches. I don't want to know what corner of Hell it crawled out of, or who the original leg belonged to, or where the rest of them was.

I jump as the food processor behind me *dings*. My pizza is ready, and frankly, I can think of nothing better than stuffing my face full of doughy carbs.

I reach up without looking, grab a slice of cheesy goodness, and stuff my face, my eyes closed, savoring the moment. *Alive. I'm alive.*

It's only after I swallow a few bites that I realize the pizza tastes wrong. Gummy. Sweet.

Opening my eyes, I already know what I'll find: my half-eaten slice of pizza, covered in neon pink.

My stomach revolts, and I vomit, spitting pink.

Too late. I can feel the gurgling in my stomach, my flesh expanding outwards, pregnant with—if the legs were any indication—myself. Fear floods my body, and I wonder which part of me was going to explode to give way to more of myself.

The rumbling moves upwards, and I know where it's heading.

"Hey, Char," I say, fear flooding my body. "You ever hear the one about the starfish girl?"

"No, Rhoda. I haven't."

I take another bite of pizza, knowing my fate is already sealed. I'd rather die happy than die hungry.

I begin to hallucinate images of my head in pinwheels, pizza gripped between my teeth. I hope whoever finds me—the many mes—enjoys their starfish pizza party.

My vision goes dark. The blackest parts of space often hold the most colorful life. As black gives way to pink, I know death isn't much different.

"They say..." My neck begins to strain, speech slurring. "They say she could never get ahea—"

My skin screams, the pink mold froths from my pores.

Bright pink.

Chapter 6
Ghoul's Kitchen

"We're going to go ahead and give that dish a solid score of four."

A dozen groans filled the audience, hands reaching toward the dishes displayed on the glass countertop under the spotlight. Mouths filled with sharp teeth salivated at the food, plated with a professional eye.

The protein was seared to perfection, sliced in thin portions the size of silver dollars. The meat swam in a puddle of au jus, rich brown and thick. A dash of parsley, reserved so as not to upset one of the judges who detested the extra flourish, sat atop the gray-pink slices.

Pale hands lifted the plate and tucked it away for future consumption. The audience members pushed their restraints to the limits, trying to catch a taste of the food on their tongues, swirling about their mouths.

"Up next, we have a dish from sous chef, Aaron Shithe. He hails from Southern California and is hoping to bring a little bit of Latin flare to his plate."

The host, a smiling woman with sparkling white teeth, held the microphone close to her mouth. Cameras circled sous chef Aaron as he put the finishing touches on his dish. Bright-red ceramic holders—designed solely for the purpose of holding tacos—appeared on the screen, piled high with pickled cabbage, chunks of mango, and chopped beer-battered bits of brain.

Human brain, the best kind.

Sous chef Aaron beamed—standing behind his plate, arms behind his back, nails digging into the palm of his other hand, leaving half-moon marks in the flesh as he awaited his score.

It had to be perfect. He needed a score of five to be able to best his opponent and take his place in the competition. Impressing the three judges was no easy feat. Their pedigree was intimidating at best, and completely demoralizing at worst, so Aaron knew his technique and flavors needed to be perfect. Not an inch of error would be accepted. He hoped his culinary training would not fail him.

The blonde judge with piercing blue eyes shook her head. Aaron's heart sunk as she opened her mouth. "Absolutely dreadful." She grimaced as though the meal was sour, offensive.

The smaller, balding man with a paunchy belly spat the food to the side in a napkin, making a show of doing so. "Undigestible. A travesty any day of the week."

The final judge, the restaurateur and Michelin-starred chef wrinkled her nose in disgust. "Take the 'h-e' out of this fellow's last name and you've got yourself exactly what this dish tastes like."

Aaron's heart may as well have been splashing about the floor by his toes, ripped out and discarded.

To put the nail in his coffin, the head judge scooped up the plate and tossed it into the audience. Moaning bodies shuffled to the discarded meal, shoveling bits of brain into their mouths as fast as they could, conveyor belts of palms whisking every last scrap into their faces.

Aaron stood in the spotlight, though instead of feeling the pride of success, the circle of light only served to highlight his shame and disappointment.

Like hamburgers that had adhered to a greasy pan, Aaron scraped his feet from the floor and shambled off-stage. For the most alive person in the studio, he felt the deadest inside.

***

"Stupid ghouls," Aaron muttered to himself outside the building that held the syndicated TV success *Ghoul's Kitchen*. "They don't even know what they want. Hot brains? Cold brains? Whole thing's rigged anyways."

Aaron kicked rocks and empty soda cans down the street, vowing to himself that he didn't need the hundred grand prize or the fancy job. He continued to grumble as he made his way back to his tiny studio apartment. "Who wants to be a chef for the ghouls anyway?"

Aaron fumbled his keys, making his way inside.

"*I* do," he conceded to himself, sighing.

He entered his apartment, the smell of the kitchen hitting him hard like a rotten fish slap in the face.

"Dammit! The brains are rotted again," he shouted to his apartment. He knew that smell, knew it meant he'd have to procure new meat before he practiced his dish some more.

"How'd it go?" a voice called from his couch, causing Aaron to jump and knock a metal spatula to the floor. A head peeked over the edge of the cloth sofa, bright pink and spiky.

"Hey Delia," Aaron replied. "You scared the crap out of me."

"Sorry, man," Delia said, biting her lip. "Well, how'd it go? You going to be America's next Monster Chef?"

"You'll find out next Tuesday." He bit back a sob.

"That bad?"

"Worse."

"Did you have to run away, hands over your ears protecting your brains so the ghouls didn't steal what's left of them?"

"Okay, maybe not that bad." Aaron let out a sad groan. "But it still sucked. They ripped the dish to shreds. Made fun of my name."

"Aw, that's low, even for a bunch of ghouls." Delia rose from her place on the couch and walked over to Aaron, wrapping her hands around his waist. "Well, the only place to go is up. And maybe to the dumpster with these rotted-out brains. Pretty rank, Aaron."

"You know you could have taken them, instead of letting them fester."

"You forget: lazy."

"Ay, there's the rub."

The two walked, hand in hand to the dumpster, a sack of spoiled brains gripped tight in Aaron's hands.

"Where am I going to get new brains?" He shook the sack, releasing a wave of fetid smells. "These were the last of my last bribe to the funeral home."

"Maybe that's the problem," Delia said. "You bring your own food preparations to the contest right? Including the brains?"

"We do," he said, stroking his hairless chin. "And I always try to bring the freshest, but maybe the brains are the problem. I'm stuck using days-old scraps. You should have seen the other plates, Delia. They were like the Kobe beef of brains, beautifully marbled. Not even a whiff of rot."

"We need to get you some better brains then."

"Smarter brains. Strong brains." Aaron smiled, an honest, real, excited smile. *Maybe Monster Chef wasn't such a pipe dream title, after all.*

***

Aaron was relieved the first steps of his plan were so easy to put into action. He'd called the studio, begged for another chance. The assistant he spoke to relayed his message to the producers and they agreed to have him back, hoping another complete demoralization of a contestant would boost their ratings.

His episode would film in two days. Another battle to get an apron and be in the running to conquer the culinary world. He had planned his recipe: a simple braised brains with shallots and a parsnip purée, beets pickled atop.

The acquisition of the brains was proving to be a bit more difficult. If Aaron and Delia's theory was correct, they needed the freshest, most potent brains around to satisfy the judges. No more brains past their expiration date.

As Aaron looked at his target through his back window—a physicist at the local college—he felt a pang of guilt. He couldn't bring himself to entertain the morality of why this person's life meant less than his dreams of success. He just knew he had goals, and TV fame and chef stardom mattered more to him than anything he could imagine.

Aaron crept toward the house, the spotlight in his mind blinding his ability to think like a human rather than a flesh-and-brain obsessed ghoul. They'd be his brains all the same.

He slid open the back door of the house, prepping the chemicals to knock out his subject. The professor entered the kitchen, humming a jaunty tune, while Aaron crouched out of sight, ducking behind the island. He heard her rummaging in a cupboard, tiptoed behind her crouched form, and pounced.

No time to scream, to fight back, only to slump into his arms, unconscious. He dragged her outside, and Delia pulled up with her car. Together they hoisted her body into the vehicle, stuffing her torso, then her legs, into the trunk as if filling a cordon bleu.

"The warehouse is ready," Delia said. She had prepared her art workspace for the professor, the solitude an artist requires coming in handy for criminal pursuits.

The two drove in silence, anticipation of their plan's imminent success or failure racing through their frantic minds. Aaron was thankful that Delia was willing to put her neck on the line for him. But she knew as well as him that art and creative pursuits were the lifeblood they both thrived on. Besides, she had plans for an art installation using pieces of the body in ways people would never guess it had once been human. Mad scientist creatives, the both of them.

They arrived at the desolate warehouse and set the professor up inside.

***

"What's the square root of forty-nine?"

"Seven."

"ABCs, backward, quick."

"What is this, a DUI test or a brain teaser?"

"Fine, the ABCs backward using the military phonetic alphabet."

"Foxtrot, Uniform, Charlie, Kilo to you."

Zap.

During the past two days, Delia and Aaron tenderized the professor's brain, pumping it full of logic problems, math, science, vocabulary, history...the list was endless and so was the cattle prod shocking when the professor refused to answer a question. The pair believed the electricity would help get the energy flowing in the mind even if the brain teasers didn't.

On the third day, Delia was lubing the professor's brain with an abundance of knowledge while Aaron prepared the ingredients for his dish. His episode was set to film that night, and he was buzzing with excitement.

He knew his dish would impress the judges. They had the culinary gift, something they retained once they transformed into ghouls, along with the entirety of a small town a few years earlier..

As soon as Aaron saw the opportunity, he knew he had to take it. No need to be chef to the stars when one could be a chef to the ghouls, always wanting more.

He reminded himself of this, over and over, as he placed his ingredients in glassware to take to the show. Reminded himself of his desire, that he deserved the best and had worked *so damn hard* to get to this point.

So hard, he thought, mallet in one hand, bone saw in another. He wouldn't let a little soft murder get in the way.

He approached the professor, steeling himself for the gore he was about to create. She screamed, he struck, he sawed, and after fifteen minutes of effort, he held her brain in his hands.

He resisted the urge to hold the brain high above him and scream in glorious victory. Not yet. Not until that apron was wrapped around his body where it belonged.

***

Delia took her place in the human section of the crowd, ready to cheer her friend to victory. Aaron proceeded through the pre-show setup, going through hair and make-up while his ingredients were placed on the show table under the spotlight.

"Brains were legally obtained?" a show manager asked Aaron.

"You bet. Here's the paperwork," Aaron replied, handing the manager the paperwork for the brains he'd previously thrown away.

"Yeesh, date's a little old there. Can't wait to see them rip you one in front of the world."

"That's what I'm here for." Aaron shrugged.

"Don't forget to sign this. Gotta make sure we're all legal here, too."

"Got a pen?"

"Here you go." The manager handed Aaron a fancy pen. "Don't forget to read closely. Make sure you're okay with it all. No small thing, you know? I honestly can't believe you're signing up for this."

"Have to make it big somehow, right? Miss all the swings you never try or whatever."

"Yeah, but like this? Human to human, there has to be a better way."

"Only way I know how," Aaron said.

The manager shrugged, his hand running through his greasy hair. "Good luck getting torn to pieces, kid."

Aaron took a deep breath, readying himself for the heat of the stage lights. He heard the theme song playing, a quartet of ghouls singing live in glittering dresses, their wispy hair falling in tatters from their leathery scalps.

"I know what ghouls like,
I know what ghouls like,
Soft-eating licorice,
Cheerios and raw fish.
I know what ghouls like,
Ghouls like, ghouls like,

Me"

The ghouls in the crowd danced to the beat, enjoying the cheery introduction. They were already drooling, smelling the brains before the aroma hit the air from the stove. They were loyal, never missing a taping, hoping for some of the best cooked brains out there. Honestly though, they'd take anything thrown their way.

The lights centered on the host, introducing the chefs for the day, urging the crowd to chant for their first guest.

"Aar-on! Aar-on!" they shouted, punctuated by gentle groans and smacking of lips.

The host smiled, flashing white pristine teeth, a contrast to the rotted mouths of the audience. "You may recognize sous chef Aaron from a week ago. He presented brains so poorly cooked that even our audience members had trouble keeping it down."

That's a lie, Aaron thought, stewing inside.

"But today, he promises he's brought us a dish we can't say no to. He thinks this plate will set him on his journey to become the next Monster Chef. Let's see if he's all talk or if he really does have the brains to get the job done."

Aaron waved to the crowd, to the camera, trying to flush away his nerves. He imagined himself putting on the black apron, feeling its soft, firm cloth wrapping around his body. He got to work.

Aaron worked his way through his dish, braising and searing the brains and puréeing his vegetables and other ingredients to a fine consistency. He prepared the plate, spreading the mash across the ceramic surface before slicing and portioning out the cooked brains.

A masterpiece, Aaron thought, pride swelling in his chest.

The judges descended upon the dish, daintily forking the meal into their mouths, skin chapped and flaking, hanging off their chins and cheeks. Their faces lit up in excitement.

The first judge, the blonde chef spoke. "This... This is incredible. Some of the best brains I've ever tasted."

The bald male chef nodded eagerly, his thin wisps of the hair he had left bobbing back and forth like dandelions in the wind. "A real turnaround from that crap he presented last week."

The final chef, notorious for being difficult to impress and known for public shaming, held her hands up, a smile creeping on her face, unable to speak. That said it all.

The host put her arms around Aaron's shoulders. Aaron felt tears of joy, sprinkling his cheeks. He was almost embarrassed but didn't deny himself the elation.

This is my dream, dammit. He laughed, in disbelief that his plan had worked. He sent a silent thank you to the professor's spirit, sure she was already haunting him for his misdeeds.

The host broke his excited frenzy by holding up a black apron to him, the *Ghoul's Kitchen* logo embroidered on the breast pocket. The brain with the knife cleaving it in two thumped under Aaron's buzzing fingertips, tracing the logo, making it feel as real as possible.

"Let's see you get that bad boy on," the host urged. "Wouldn't want to make too much of a mess on your nice clothes, now would we?"

Mess? Aaron stood suddenly still, confused. *Isn't the cooking over?*

"We've got a special treat for you all tonight. This dish was too good to share with our steadfast audience, but they still need to eat. We promised you a healthy serving of brain and we don't ever disappoint."

Aaron felt his stomach drop. He tried to remember back to his contract, but the crowd of hungry eyes and greedy moans made it hard to think. What did I make legal? What did I sign away?

The host shot her hand out and grabbed Aaron by the throat.

My life. I signed away my life.

"We have a new segment of the show tonight. Not just a live taping, but a live *feeding*. What do you say my ghoulfiends, are you in?"

The crowd cheered in a symphony of undead moans.

Aaron looked to the rafters, to the human section of the audience. Their faces looked shocked, scared, among them, Delia's. Aaron could see the tears sparkling in the light as they ran down her face.

The host grabbed a mallet from Aaron's table. It still glimmered with the professor's brain, as he had used it to tenderize his dish only minutes earlier.

She swung. The mallet connected with a muffled *thump* and Aaron dropped like a sack of beans to the ground. He twitched, his body barely able to move under his commands. His fingers grazed the apron wrapped around his torso, trying to find some final sense of accomplishment amidst his twist of fate.

The host cackled, swung again, and cracked his head open.

His world went black, even as the spotlight stayed on his head, gray matter spilling to the floor, only to be scooped up by the host and tossed into the audience.

"How about some brains tartare?" she yelled as the crowd tripped over themselves to get to the mashed bits of Aaron being tossed into the sea of bodies.

As Aaron faded away, he heard the theme song for *Ghoul's Kitchen* playing in his head.

I know what ghouls like,
Ghouls like, ghouls like.
Me.
And oh, how they did.

Chapter 7
Surrender, Slowly Baked

I baked in that room, the one you made for me.

A relationship takes compromise, and I was elated to be with you. I told you I was happy to play in your kitchen, by your rules, to sit and fester in my reality while navigating yours. That closet, cardboard in construction, heat radiating, became my oven. Walls up, heat on. Pre-heated, whirlwind intensity. Love.

A year in, I became aware of the change, my fingers pressed into spongy skin. Pores had grown larger—enough to house a grub—but empty, caving in under my touch. Just a patch at first, a couple of square inches of skin tunneling into paper thin burrows. I expected it to hurt, wondered what others saw when they looked at me. Was I whole?

I poked the surface, watching my finger press deep to the bone, skin edging over the tip of my nail. Polish made of crusty membranes. A new veneer. Earlier that week you told your mom I was your room-mate, even though we've kissed daily for a year now. I'll keep my new skin to be able to continue kissing you.

A few months later, it's more than just the surface now. I feel the batter concocted from a recipe passed down to you settling into my blood, making it thicker. The viscous liquid has caused my veins to widen, tunneling beneath the surface. It's better that way—the heat will move more through me smoother than ever.

I went to that office party you begged me to attend. Your colleagues—they seemed nice enough—were hassling you about asking the new guy on a date. I stood next to you, my hands in my pockets, wondering what you had told them I was to you. I was used to being the girl who had nothing better to do on a Saturday night than go to a bar with people I don't know and who wouldn't know me.

Your friends guffawed. I nodded, laughed, felt my throat grow tight. I wondered if the blood-batter was rising, if I'd bake a little more that night. I choked it down. I'll keep the cake to myself for now. These aren't the people you've chosen to share me with in that way. More slices for me. I'll grow.

I say grow, but I mean transform. Change. Cook a little more. I've become weirdly comfortable here in this oven you've made for me. Don't forget to close the door while I'm in here. My bake will be more even that way.

Your dad dropped by the other day to fix the sink when you weren't home. Asked how I was holding down the fort. I did as you desired and kept him from the master bedroom, the bed ruffled on both sides where we slept, shelled into one another last night. He cracked a few jokes. Made me—the roommate and best friend—laugh. A strange sound that forced its way through the batter in my throat. He walked straight to the pipes where the water was dripping, past our room. He didn't spare a glance at my closet, my oven on the way. He didn't know to look.

Two years in. I asked you if you'd ever tell. If I'd ever get to be yours in front of the people that matter to you.

"Someday," you said. "I'm just not ready now."

I wonder if you'll ever be ready. I tell myself you will be.

Another six months. The recipe is still being worked inside of me. I'll be the best cake. Your cake. The one you shaped with your hands, your heart. Your hands are covered in flour and I'm all mixed up. My skin flakes, remaining hollowed. I can see the thick blood-batter welling on the surface.

I'm ready to be the sweet dessert you've designed. I know I'm not who I was before, but I am who you want me to be. I'm on my side in the oven, scorching red zigzags around me. I try to smile, try not to burn. I don't scream as the heat bubbles my skin, blisters a fine layer of char. I hope it smooths out so you can smear on the frosting later.

I cook inside. My skin opens, red rolls out thick like ooze from boils left unattended. I coat myself in what's inside. It's as pretty as you wanted, I think.

You'll find me in there at some point. Reach your hands inside, pull me out and put me on the plate. You'll take your fork, examine me for the bite you've been waiting for. Your favorite flavor—everything you wanted me to be.

I don't move. Can't. I'll be trapped in this tin for as long as you'll have me. Fully baked, your fork dipping in over and over, taking pieces of me into your mouth. I suppose it's not cannibalism if I'm no longer human.

To be with you I only had to give up all that I was. A surrender, slowly baked.. I'd do it again, if there was anything but crumbs of me left.

Chapter 8
Escargot, Except It's You

I married my current wife Natalia not out of love, but because she possessed access to something I needed.

That makes me a shitty person, I get it. She doesn't know any better, and I keep her happy, so I think I'm doing okay. Living just above the moral low-ground, maybe.

I remember when she asked me, she said, "Maura, you love me right?" and before I responded, I didn't think of her. Instead, I conjured up an imaginary plate, adorned with the salty morsel I craved. There it was, the missing link of the dish I'd tried to perfect my whole life, and I said, "Yes, I do." I loved the idea of that snail, even if I didn't love Natalia.

She was a fine woman. But what made her finer was her career. Not her driven personality and strong work ethic. I mean, those things are good, I guess. They got her to where she is. But really, it's what she does. Where she goes.

Like today, for example. Today, she goes where I've needed her to since the days before we even met.

Today, she goes to the bottom of the Japan Trench.

And I go with her.

I'd been following her research for years. Found an article on the web about her attempted journeys to reach the bottom of the ocean. Saw a picture of her in her thick-rimmed glasses and tight ponytail, looking every bit the part of the scientist she is. I didn't care that her deep brown eyes smiled at the edges, and that her mouth was a beautiful rose pink with perfect white teeth nestled within. I didn't care that she was independently wealthy, donated to charity, and happened to be smart as shit.

Those might have been the things that made her someone else's dream woman. But me? I cared about two things. She gay? Tick. I'd have a shot at getting her to fall in love with me. I scanned that article, read something about an ex-wife, and figured that was my money made.

But that second box was more important, and Natalia ticked it twice. *What* she does with that brain. *How* she spends that money. She's a deep-sea specialist, on the cutting edge of mapping the oceanic terrain. Spends her time with a team of engineers, all sorts of science-y stuff that's supposed to be able to allow her to travel in a submersible thousands of meters deep.

She's going to put that little ship to the test today. 8,000 meters, to the bottom of the Japan Trench. And there, when she grabs her sediment sample, I'm going to send every prayer I know to whatever god there is that she takes a handful of the fabled trench snail with it. And I'll pray a little more that I can sneak one away from her lab once it's there. And maybe one more that I don't completely fuck up preparing it for the dish I want to present at my restaurant that'll earn me my first Michelin star.

So here we are. She's in the submersible. I'm in her lab.

She's getting ready to go below surface. Her little team is out there on the docks with her, fluffing her up as she gets ready to do the unthinkable and go where nobody has before. Down into the deep. One of the deepest places in the world.

The bottom of the Japan Trench.

No one knows what to expect. Up until this point, people have only collected chemical samples from the flumes around the trench. Only have *suggestions* of what might be there. Life, they guess. Nutrient-rich sediment that can support life. That's what science *suggests*.

But the stories... Those are a whole different kind of suggestion. Fishermen, divers, folkloric tales... All of them say there *is* life down there. That on the bottom of the sea floor lies thousands of crawling, fist-sized, sacred snails. Their shells are made of igneous rock, formed by the magma that isn't much further below the trench. The deeper you go, the more delicious life is. I'm betting my own life that these snails are edible, and that they will make me a star chef.

This snail means the world to me. I just know that it's what I need to bring my restaurant to the next level. To bring that bit of exoticism to the plate that no one else can achieve. That it's going to taste like a dream served boiled, seasoned just right, looking beautiful with that shell of hardened magma glistening on the plate.

The chatter on the comms cuts through the thick syrupy sweetness of my dreams.

Lana, Natalia's best friend and lead engineer, mumbles, "Can't believe it's happening, boss."

Natalia's voice is clear as day despite the thick Plexiglass and titanium surrounding her. "Just a quick look-see is all we're doing today. Nothing too sensational." She's humble. She *better* be doing more than just looking. I need her to be grabbing too.

"And taking samples, right?" I ask.

"Not today, Maura."

My heart drops with those three words. I... I've waited so long for this day. To get these snails.

She continues. "We won't be ready for retrieval for another couple of months. We need to know what we're looking at before we know what to take."

I roll my eyes in the safety of the empty lab. How scientifically...quaint.

In this moment, I have decisions to make. My restaurant and career was languishing in the mundane. Over the last few months, I'd managed to grab the attention of some great chefs and critics and I wouldn't be able to hold onto them for much longer. I'd heard talk of iron-enriched, decadent vegetables from a farm out west, evidence of a ticking time-bomb before people move onto the next culinary powerhouse. I need to get this dish out—this dish that nobody in the world could replicate—and I needed it out now. Not enough time on Natalia's timeline. Months? I barely have weeks to make something happen in today's climate.

So, I make my first decision.

"Natalia? I'm getting some weird signals in the lab here."

She's silent.

"Uh, some weird beeping and red lights on the exo of your sub," I continue, attempting to make it sound important. "You might want to send the crew."

Natalia sighs. "Fine. Lana, Boyd, head on back."

"Roger, boss."

I find a wrench and it's hefty and cold in my hands.

After a few minutes, Boyd and Lana enter the lab, heading straight for the computer.

"I don't hear anything," Boyd says, his voice a rumble.

"The lights were just on the monitor, I swear," I say.

Lana and Boyd huddle around the computer, eyes squinting against the light of the screen. Lana turns to me. "Maura, I'm not seeing the—"

The wrench in my hand answers, the dull thud of the metal against her skull overtaking the gasp that escapes her mouth as her head caves in. The blow to her temple sends her to her knees. Boyd swivels only to meet the clawed fingers of the wrench, this time from a backhand I send his way. The force is hard enough to get through his thick skull, splitting his head open in an arc of red.

He doesn't move again. Lana sputters on the ground. I strike her again, pushing the sound of her crushed face from my mind, my thoughts aimed only at the thought of what the trench holds.

With the two crew members disposed of, I make my way to the bay. The hammering of my heart covers the soft plinking of the blood as it falls from the lips of the wrench to the metal hallway below.

I hear Natalia asking for responses in my earpiece. "What's going on with the ship?" She's persistent. "Lana? Boyd?" And after a few beats: "Maura?"

"Just coming to help them run a diagnostic. I'll see you in a second."

And I do. Around the corner, floating in the docking bay, is my wife, surrounded by the thick Plexiglass dome of the submersible. It's a small craft, just large enough for a single person to move around, with a set of arms and storage on the underside. Cameras are mounted on the exterior, tiny lights blinking, ready to record history.

Can't let them record me.

"Hey, honey, can you power down for a minute? Something weird was going on and you should take a look at it inside."

She looks at me, love in her eyes, and I feel a twinge of guilt at her inevitable demise. She had big dreams, the brains to achieve them, but a heart that couldn't see through my bullshit. She was blind to being used. I tell myself it's not my fault, that she should have known I was no good.

Natalia steps out of the craft. She really is beautiful, fit and youthful, full of energy. I almost wish I had room in my own heart for her. But cooking—my passion—it really takes it all. I could either have the love of my life, or a life worth living.

"Maura, is everything okay?" Her innocent voice pulls at whatever feelings I have for her.

"Just fine, Natalia," I say, my voice below a whisper as I wrap her in a hug. My eyes catch the sight of the name painted onto the sub. *Maura's Sub Sandwich*. I hate that pun. I hate that she named it after me.

She doesn't see the wrench as my arms curve around her.

She won't get me what I need, so I have to get it myself. I make my last decision.

I turn her body, pull it close to mine. Lifting the wrench to her neck, I grab both sides and pull. The metal crushes her hyoid, and it isn't long before she suffocates.

The sub is open and waiting for me to drive her to the bottom of the ocean.

Who knows how long I'll have until someone finds the bodies. I don't know how long I'll have down there. I push Natalia's body to the edge of the dock, roll her over the side and into the water. I want her to sink, to reach the depths of the ocean so she can achieve her dreams of being at the bottom of the trench. I'm not a complete monster, you know.

A panel of buttons of levers greet me as I hop into the sub and close the hatch. It looks self-explanatory enough. The design is sleek, and I send a silent thank you to the dead engineers in the control room lab for making the craft as simple as possible to drive.

I take a breath, almost as if I'm dunking my head in a swimming pool, and flip the switch that powers the sub. It whirs to life, and I exhale, hearing the energy thrum through the machine.

My instincts take over, and before I know it, I'm maneuvering the sub below the surface, marveling at how easy this is. Maybe Natalia wasn't as smart as I gave her credit for. Or maybe I was just as good as her.

Down and down I go, attempting to follow the HUD to the Japan Trench. As far as I can tell, the coordinates and depth are plugged into the machine, making navigation smooth as butter. I cut through the blue of the ocean, leaving behind my worries and guilt in a gentle stream of bubbles. My path scribbles an etch-a-sketch into the water, memories of every meter I descend carved into the depths.

I wonder if anything will know to follow.

For the first hundred meters of the mile long descent, the life was plentiful. Fish, jellies, bigger fish, sharks, seaweed... Nothing out of the norm. I didn't need them. I needed to go deeper.

The display tells me I'm headed for treasure. Minutes feel like hours in the quiet pass. It's been dark for a while now. Nothing but the lights of the ship, though they land on nothing, as far as I can tell. I no longer wonder when I'll see the trench. I realize now, here in the dark that there isn't anything to see. No sign welcoming you to the black depths.

I am the trench. In it. Swallowed by her mouth, which stretches in every direction.

Here, alone, I wonder if the snails are worth it. This feeling of insignificance in the endless dark. The death. Will I die?

Chiding myself for my recklessness, I realize I don't know what the hell I'm doing. That I have just murdered my wife and her crew and commandeered a sub I've never piloted to find some snails—which might not even exist—at the bottom of the ocean which may or may not be edible and may or may not change my life forever so long as I get away with the crimes I've committed.

I begin to panic, the blackness around me screaming, slinging insults into my face. Every inch of obsidian water that passes my window tells me I'm a goddamn idiot.

But I am a goddamn idiot and with only a thousand meters before I reach the bottom. A goddamn idiot who hasn't yet exploded from the immense amount of pressure threatening to crush me and the sub. A goddamn idiot who was putting a helluva lot of faith in a self-guiding watercraft built outside the government domain, funded with private dollars and whole barrels full of gumption.

Another ten minutes of miserable, silent thinking, and I arrive. I feel the sub slow, hover, extend its legs and settle into the sand or rock or whatever makes up the floor. The cameras relay a feed to the HUD, the lights powering up at full force.

When the lights go up, my whole world changes.

The blackness that stretched for miles in every direction sees a spotlight it has never before experienced. In that moment, I grasp what I've done. I've taken over one of the greatest deep-sea accomplishments for what... Snails? Which, now that the light was on, I didn't even see.

The dark void may have disappeared in the light, but the emptiness remained.

At the bottom of the trench, I am truly at my lowest of lows.

Unless...

The sand ahead agitates. A small eruption of silt clouds the floor, and I find myself holding my breath again, not wanting to make sound.

A rock breaks the sand's top layer. It pushes up, rounded, jagged, as if the ocean floor is birthing land right before my eyes. Pushing toward the sky, wherever it is, to get up from the depths, such a strange concept to my brain which just spent the better part of an hour descending into the black.

The rock breaches, about a foot in diameter, followed by an electric green, gyrating mound of flesh, smooth as a marble.

I exhale, resisting the urge to scream.

It's a fucking snail. It's *the* snail.

Prayers, answered.

The snail stops, looks around on its stalk eyes, and I wonder if it can sense the light, the way its home is exposed.

It must not notice, or care, as it moves forward. I contemplate sending the arms of the sub to grab it, but stop when I see the rising sand clouds from dozens of other spots in front of me. I glance at the back cameras and can see them all around me.

Hundreds of the most exotic snails on Earth, heading right for me.

I can't hold out any longer, seeing the wealth of the gods in front of me. I press a button, grab the joystick that controls the arms of the sub. *Just like the video games*, I think, extending the arms to menace over the closest snail. I grab it.

The arms retreat to the sub, placing it in the storage below. I try to discern how many I can take, filling the stomach of the ship one by one until the display tells me it's beyond capacity.

I feel a gnawing in my gut, wishing I could grab more, not knowing if I'll ever get this chance again.

I take another snail into the arms of the sub, determined to carry it out just like that on my way up. I maneuver the claw so I can see it right in front of the window of the ship. The snail, with its bulbous feelers and vibrant skin, appears to be staring back at me.

Ugly, beautiful, *perfect*.

I try to imagine it boiling in a pot, try to picture the seasonings I'd pepper onto its skin. Paint a divine portrait of its glorious bright skin and shining, rocky shell on a plate. I visualize holding that plate, smiling in a picture, an article about my Michelin star award.

The snail stopped wiggling in the claw of the ship. I wonder if I killed it.

Before I can set it down to grab another, it opens a mouth—*Where did it get a mouth from?*

The snail screams.

The sonic shout penetrates the thick walls of the sub. I raise my hands to try and halt the sound—a futile attempt, I realize—as my hands feel the wetness of blood trickling from my ears. The scream alerts the snails within the belly of the ship's storage. They start to yell in synchronicity with its brethren.

I feel like I'm vibrating out of my mind. My skin—god, my skin! Its vacillating in wild waves, blurred by the motion of the snail's movement back and forth. It's flaying me alive.

My eyeballs feel like a mound of Jell-O, flicked by some kid who'd rather play with his food than eat it. I try to see through the constant movement, try to find the switch to start the ship back on its course to the surface. My fingers find the button. Taking all the damn energy I have to push it.

The screaming stops before I can press the button.

I breathe, thankful that the torturous noise has ceased. My body feels like it went twenty rounds with a steel pole, every inch buzzing.

I raise my eyes back out to the window. See the snail has tucked into its shell.

The rumbling begins.

All around me the sand builds like a fog. It feels like the ground beneath the sub's legs is cracking and shifting, and I pray that an oceanic earthquake hasn't been triggered. Minutes of tremors and complete sand-filled blindness has me babbling commands at the controls. The sensors on the ship are going off, sending stabs of pain behind my eyes, still recovering from the sonic shrills of the snails.

I think of Natalia and her broken throat and I know I deserve this hell.

When the dust settles, I wish for the ground to swallow me.

In front of the ship, in front of me, is a snail that defies nature. Towering over me, at least forty feet tall, it looms. The boulder that is its shell feels impossibly large—like a moon I expect to begin orbiting.

Electric green—just like what I now realize to be the infantile sea snails I carried in the stomach of my ship.

With one look into what I assume is its blobby, ill-defined face, I know I'm fucked.

My fingers stab the button to send the seacraft into ascension, thinking I can blink the hell out of here before that snail can punish me for stealing its children. Nothing happens, except more sirens and a flashing light indicating that the ship is too heavy to properly rise.

We won't be ready for retrieval for another couple of months. Natalia's words echo in the ocean deep.

Fuck this. These snails might have been worth the collateral damage of Natalia and her crew, but not my own. I move to release the sea snails I've captured. Leave them behind, for now.

I could always come back. I could always—

The giant snail shifts. It snorts from nostrils I cannot see—*do snails even snort?*—and a cavernous mouth opens in what I thought was its chest.

The hole is lined with teeth like stalactites.

"Take them back!" I yell, jamming my finger into the storage release over and over again.

Even as I feel the snails fall from the ship, I know it wants more. Not just its babies. Revenge. I interrupted its sleep. Its peaceful whatever-the-fuck kind of life it had here at the bottom of the trench.

With the ship relieved of the precious cargo, I stab the flight button again. The sub begins to whirr, readying itself for ascent. I cry as I feel the arms and legs of the ship tuck back into the hull.

The ship hovers.

"Hurry up, you sonuvabitch! Go!"

It doesn't care that I'm sobbing as the humongous snail opens its mouth wider. It moves. So. Damn. Slowly.

The monstrous snail's mouth turns to a snarl. It opens again, this time sucking in with all its might. A vortex appears before it, and my ship, even with its attempt at ascent, struggles against the current.

Everything is loud and crushing metal as I whirl through the chasm of the sea, ever closer to the snail.

Everything is pressure as the sub strikes the dangling teeth of the snail's mouth.

Everything is pain as the ship crumbles under the weight of the ocean.

I explode from the ship, broken, beaten, bloody.

Light disappears as the sub is destroyed. In blackness again, this time, inside the mouth of the very creature I longed to retrieve. I'm pretty sure I'm dying fast.

I wonder if the snail would have been edible raw. I wonder if the snail would have preferred me to be cooked. My ship was a beautiful shell, I think.

Chapter 9
Mycelium
Ouroboros

Field Note, December 17th, 2009
Location: No way I'm telling you, but just so I know: it's that place near the trees that look a bit like your Aunt Helen and her husband.

The forest is screaming today.

Birds, loud and angry that I'm trampling deep into the folds of their homes. The air, hot despite the incoming winter. I am not to be deterred though. The ground is soft, the hairs on my arm are standing tall, pointing me up and away from the forest floor where I should be scouting.

These truffles won't find themselves.

In all my years hunting the decadent fungus, I haven't hit it big yet. But I know I can do it. I'm capable. I don't need a dog or a pig. I have me, and my sensibility.

This is my year. My harvest. I'm here to fill my bags with expensive dirt.

If I have to rake this forest empty, I will.

And maybe that's why the woods are screaming today. The metal rake is firm in my hands, and I can hear the birds calling out my treason. It's like they're yelling "Josie, Josie, you know that what you're about to do will wreck the floor of these woods for cycles to come. Be less destructive, Josie. Do it for Hannah, Josie."

How they know the name of my wife is beyond me, but that's what I'm convinced they're yelling. But like I said before, I won't be deterred.

The teeth of my rake digs into the dirt, and I can almost hear the roots of trees and ferns and bushes groaning and snapping against the metal prongs. The resistance only makes me dig deeper, hoping to grab the delectable fungus in the mouth of the rake.

I can cover more ground this way. Make my days shorter. And no one cares but the forest, and she can't really talk so I'm going to plow until I can make my $300 for the day.

The birds continue to scream. I continue to hunt. The sun begins to set.

I'll be back tomorrow.

***

Field Note, December 19th, 2009

Location: Half mile north from Aunt Helen and her husband. Look for the rock that smells like shit.

I didn't write yesterday because my hands were too raw from the raking. The skin still burns and stings today, but I have to document what I just found.

I'd raised the earth of almost a football field worth of forest floor. The days only churned a handful of worthwhile fungus. None of the best stuff, but something at least to keep the wolves at bay so the bills get paid, and Hannah can stay at home and write her book for a little while longer.

But about five minutes ago, I found it. It sat in a spotlight of yellow rays, filtered through the dense thicket of trees like a goddamned scene from a fairytale. Glimmering under the sun, the ring appeared.

A ring of mushrooms.

I don't see them often. In fact, I haven't seen them at all in this stretch of the woods, now that I think about it. Not in this forest, where the fog lies dense during the day and the birds scream obscenities at you.

This forest, which I thought would yield the truffles I needed because, let's be real, it looked haunted as shit. So haunted that I didn't think other people would come out here and all the unearthed bundles of fungal gold would be mine.

No one wants to rupture the earth in a haunted forest. No one wants to disturb that soil. So yeah, the fog, the bird screams, the distinct lack of people—

And now, a fairy ring of mushrooms.

All the truffle-hunting science points to these circles of mushrooms as being indicative of lush soil, ripe with truffles. You see 'em, you start digging.

So I did. I examined the three-yard diameter, followed the circumference of the circle, closed my eyes and started the search. Tried to sniff out the rich scent I told myself I could detect. Put my arms out like a dowsing rod.

And there, at the center, I clawed the dirt away from midpoint of the circle and unearthed perfect lumps of dirt...

Truffles. Rotted to the core.

The birds laughed at me.

I laughed back, throwing fetid truffles at the trees.

As the brown shapes arced across the sky, I could see the darkness creeping in.

The only thing worse than a haunted forest is being in one at night. Even I'm not brave enough for that.

**

Field Note, December 20ᵗʰ, 2009
Location: Back at that godforsaken rock.

I found the spot I left yesterday. Followed the lines I'd dragged in the dirt with my metal rake to lead me back the next day.

I had a bone to pick with this part of the forest.

I had truffles to force from the earth.

The woods aren't really haunted, you know. Don't want to mislead my notes here with my hyperbolic take of the creeping eyes of the forest and my overblown courage. I don't actually think there are ghosts here.

But the trees, this dirt, and most specifically, this fairy ring have haunted my thoughts all night. Called me back with a whispering, slithering voice.

Hannah had asked how things were going, her eyes red from hours spent at the computer. I lied and told her I was going to strike it big. I stood, guilt in my throat like a knot in a log.

I'm back at this fairy ring today to make it bleed. Make it weep with truffles. Make it undo my lie, make it a truth.

I've spent the last hour searching the soil around the ring, my nose practically to the dirt. The birds are laughing, I know, at my ass pointed skyward. I've given them the finger several times already, but it hasn't shut them up.

My frustration is mounting, and it's taking all my will not to break my rake over this goddamned ring of mushrooms, their rounded tips pointing at me, like kids in a classroom who've found their mark to ridicule.

A blister on my hand pops, and so does my ability to contain myself. I step to the center of the ring, and I start wailing on these assholes, these laughing fungi.

I swing and bash and my arms start to buckle and I look at my destruction and see the chunks of white mushrooms scattered about. No longer a ring. Just pieces of trash on a trash floor of a trash forest.

I throw my rake on the floor.

I leave.

***

Field Note, December 21st, 2009
  Location: Rock.

I tried to forget the ring, but I needed to go back. It sang circles of rot in my brain all night. Hannah had to repeat herself several times to be heard over the cacophony of fungal hymns in my head.

I had to come back. Plus, I left my rake in the spot, and I really like that rake and I can't afford another one. So here I am, at the scene of my destruction, except it's not destruction anymore.

Where once dozens of mushrooms lay broken like little bastards on the floor of the forest, the circle has returned. Fuller than before.

I rub my eyes, then chide myself for touching my face with my dirt-ridden hands.

I blink.

The ring is still there, right next to my rake which had ripped the circle to shreds the day before.

Maybe the forest *is* haunted.

I shake myself from my stupor, reach forward to grab my rake at the center of the mushroom ring. I cross the threshold.

Don't cross it again.

I'm still here, stuck in the center of the ring with my notebook, my pen, and my rake, and it's all I can do to document what happens in case someone follows those lines to my place in the woods.

But the change is already taking place, so I'm not sure how much good it will do.

My feet are rooted to the center, my shoes flush against the earth. About thirty minutes ago, I felt a tingling in my soles, then a worming of flesh through the rubber of my shoes digging deep into the soil. I screamed and the birds laughed back at me.

It took a bit to regain my composure. No matter how hard I pulled against the ground, my feet wouldn't move from their spots, like they'd become a part of an ancient root structure. And to try and tear away felt like it was ripping tendons from my muscles and bones. I was pulled taut, snapping back to the ground.

The woods are crying for my blood, just as I had tried to bleed it dry. The ring of mushrooms have traveled from their place around me, diving under me, through me.

I'm becoming it. The fungus. The ring feeding on itself. Feeding me. Pulling me through it and back out to the ring. It stands taller than it did before.

I can feel the change climbing up my legs, up my torso, and I begin to cry when it reaches my chest. I lift my shirt, seeing the white rubbery tube I've become.

My body, a mushroom stalk.

My neck, fast turning into the gills, my skin structured mycelium.

I've been like this for another ten minutes.

My body burns and all I can think about is how I'm becoming death. How I'm becoming a part of the decomposition chain.

How I'm becoming the very thing I hunt: a treasure in the soil. I vaguely consider that my bones will not be worth their weight in truffles. No time to write more. Tell you how much this hurts.

I can smell myself rot.

Arms are tubes. Pen is heavy. Brain is fuzzy. Eyes dark.

I hope Hannah finishes her book.

***

Field notes from the notebook of Josie Danielson. Found by Park Ranger Dylan. To be filed with Ms. Danielson's Missing Persons Report. Park Ranger Dylan includes the following notes with his report and this notebook:

"When I arrived at the site, I saw the forest floor had been raked recently, presumably by the metal rake found near the notebook of Josie Danielson. Ms. Danielson was nowhere to be found. No footsteps led away from the site. Other items gathered included a pile of clothing, recently worn and a bag half-filled with various types of fungi.

What I'm about to include in this report is odd, but I want to be diligent. I hope any information might lead to Ms. Danielson's return. Perhaps someone in the area is selling what I'm about to describe.

Around the pile of clothes was a ring of mushrooms. White, flecked with some red. Haven't seen this species before, uniform in their growth. The most remarkable thing, how they stood almost at attention. A plump bottom, small tubes dangling from their gills. A second lump on top. Two more tubes flopping from their sides. Humanoid in their shape.

I took a sample, which I have bagged to be filed with this report. There was no sign of a struggle."

Chapter 10
Bear Hang

C onnie opened her eyes. That feeling washed over her—waking up, but desperate to fall back to sleep for a few more greedy moments. She fought the urge to sleep, not wanting to waste a second of her time in the woods with her friends, Richie and Marla, who were celebrating their recent engagement.

She smiled, pleased that she had opted for the deluxe tent with plenty of room for her camping needs. She figured the only way to make the outdoors tolerable was to make it feel as much like the great indoors as possible.

Connie's mouth watered at the scent of savory sausages, cooking with the delicious hiss and sizzle.

She flipped the switch on her portable white noise machine and prepared to greet the day. Connie unzipped the thick tent flap and pushed through the entryway, making it no more than a couple of steps before stopping in her tracks.

Connie's blood drained from her face and a panic ignited her heartbeat into a frenzy. Crouched around the fire were two strangers with the oddest of grins, a mug of coffee held between their hands.

Staring them down, Connie heard a faint dripping beside her.

She turned toward the noise. Connie eyes bulged as she took in the space beside her gargantuan tent and saw two sleeping bags hanging from the tree with a thick rope tied around the middle of the heavy forms, knotted over a sturdy branch above. Blood had pooled in the fabric at the bottom, contributing to the growing puddle below—Richie and Marla.

"Ah! Morning!" the closer of the two strangers greeted Connie. With his face turned toward hers, she could see the buildup of grime on his skin, dirt caked on his chin and cheeks like a five o'clock shadow. He rested his coffee mug on the small camping table next to him, wiped his hands on the thigh of his cargo shorts.

"Appreciate you letting us crash yer beautiful campsite!" He continued, glee in his voice. "My wife and I here, we saw you pullin' in with all yer fancy camp gear and thought, well, I'll be. That looks like it musta cost a fortun'!"

The man took a step toward Connie, and it was then she saw the still-wet red wings of blood around the cuffs of his shirt, his hands stained by her friends' viscera. His wife had similar markings of the savagery.

As the pair moved closer to Connie, who stood frozen in disbelief, Connie chanced a glance to the fire and her Grill-dor Deluxe. The spicy scent of sausage reached her nostrils.

The grimy man continued stepping closer, the fetid smell of his breath and body fast overpowering the smell of the cooking meat.

"I hope ya don't mind Tilly and I usin' some of yer...amenities 'ere. I apologize for my appearance—we had a mighty busy morning, what with meeting yer pals and all. They acquainted us right here to yer tools and such. Was just gunna finish up brekkie here and then 'op in your portable shower. Whatchu call that thing, Tilly?"

"The Power Shower, Mac."

"Right, the Power Shower. Anyhoot, pardon me manners. I imagine yer Connie? Yer friends had a few things to say 'boutcha before they went'n got, er, tied up." He gestured to the sleeping bags, tied to the round tree branch, hanging by two sturdy, knotted ropes, the plinking of droplets of thick blood never ending. "Now, wud ya mind helpin' a man with this fancy-pants stuff?"

"Wh-what do you want?" Connie's voice wavered.

"I jus told ya what I want, girlie. Need a lil help with this 'ere shower. After that, we'll be onnerway."

Connie took a few hesitant steps toward the Power Shower, its oblong form standing across the campsite. "Just help with the shower? Then you'll let me go?"

Mac sighed. "A lil help with the shower, then maaaaybe wecun enjoy sum brekkie t'gether. You rich folk really make the saltiest meals. Gout for weeks after eating one of ya!"

Tilly scuttled over to the cooking sausage and picked up a link with her long campfire fork. She held the meat to her mouth, blew on it, and extended her arm to Connie. "Try it, Connie. You've never experienced friendship quite like this."

As Tilly approached Connie with the meat, Mac inched closer, a large knife tight in his hand. "Eat it, Connie." He menaced. "Eat it or..." He gestured with the tip of his knife toward the sleeping bags.

Connie tried to run. She made it three paces before the knife, launched from Mac's hand, penetrated the back of her thigh. She screamed, shrill and frantic.

Tilly advanced as Connie lay sprawled on the ground. In one swift motion, Tilly shoved the pronged utensil, sausage still attached, into Tilly's open mouth. The meat thunked against Connie's lips, but the fork kept going, exiting the back of Connie's neck, just under her skull.

That's... That's no sausage, Connie thought as Marla's spiced and grilled finger dangled from her lips, wedding ring still perched atop her digit. She heard the cackle of the intruding couple and everything faded.

Tilly and Mac dismembered Connie and tossed the uneaten parts of her body across the campsite along with what was left of her friends. The couple left the campsite, retreating back to their home, hidden in the woods, with their bellies full and a few new camping gadgets in their possession. They laughed, sure the park rangers would blame the carnage on a bear, desperate not to feed the rumors of the Glamping Garrotters, who always strike again.

Tilly and Mac knew one day they'd have to stop their rampage, but until then, there was always the next fancy meal to look forward to.

Chapter 11
Tuna Cans and the American Way

T he following reports were located in a drawer in the manager's office of the Shover's Valley cannery. These incident reports, which were detailed by health supervisor Hannah Lee, were taken in by local law enforcement after our investigative reporters unveiled them. We have them reprinted here in their entirety so citizens of Shover's Valley can witness the horrors the cannery was responsible for. We do so to raise awareness about the manager and owner of Shover's Valley cannery, Kevin Barnes, so he may be located and brought to justice.

***

Incident Report #1055
 2/17/1998, 5:00 p.m.
 Injury requiring medical attention
 Injured party: Matalie Jude

The following report is compiled through witness statements concerning the missing digits on the left hand of a Ms. Matalie Jude. According to witness reports, at approximately 4:45 p.m., a shout rang out through the floor of the cannery. Several workers noted the machine responsible for placing the lids on the cans of tuna was making a horrible grinding noise, "as if someone had placed a tire iron in a garbage disposal".

The first worker to arrive at the cannery, Jackson Reeves (JR), approached the scene and found Ms. Jude pale as a sheet on the floor, droplets of blood around her form, holding her hand to her chest. After coaxing her hand forward, JR noticed the source of blood which was three missing fingers—all but her thumb and pinky fingers—"ripped savagely" from her hand.

According to Ms. Jude, the machine was not loaded properly nor the conveyor belt at the correct speed. She reached to the tuna cans on the belt, and the arm that sealed the cans malfunctioned and pressed her fingers into the contents of the vessel before stamping a lid over top, severing her digits.

Ms. Jude is uncertain why the machine malfunctioned.

Ms. Jude was taken to Shover's Valley hospital for treatment. Workers are sifting through the processed cans for her missing digits, but they have yet to be found.

End incident report.

***

Incident Report #1057
  2/20/1998, 4:55 p.m.

Injury requiring medical attention; factory shutdown required
Injured party: Percy Richardson

Upon routine inspection of tuna cans in Section D of the facility, excess blood was found in product. After tracing product through the factory, worker Shay Jennings located Mr. Percy Richardson unconscious, draped over the tuna processing vat.

Mr. Richardson is currently undergoing treatment at Shover's Valley hospital, but I have been informed by the medical professionals that he should make a full recovery. They suspect he may have suffered severe food poisoning.

Workers are now pulling product exposed to Mr. Richardson's biohazard material.

After interviewing colleagues who ate lunch with Mr. Richardson, colleagues suggest that lunch was not likely the culprit for his sickness. Several workers shared soup from the local grocer, and no one else was affected.

When asked if anything happened during the lunch break, several colleagues mentioned that Manager/Owner Kevin Barnes had stopped by to check progress on the line. They noted Mr. Richardson had stayed behind to ask Mr. Barnes a question about a co-worker who had not showed up to work in over a week. Employees could not remember who he was asking about as they worked in a separate wing of the facility as Mr. Richardson.

Due to Mr. Barnes' presence, workers felt pressured to return to the line, and many cut their lunch breaks short.

Personal note: There appears to be a general unrest among the workers today. While injuries occur as part of this occupation, two in less than a week coupled with Mr. Barnes' untimely visit has workers beginning to show signs of being on edge. Requesting a factory-wide meeting to boost morale.

End incident report.

***

Incident Report #1060
2/27/1998, 5:10 p.m.
Injury requiring medical attention
Injured party: Jackie Rose

The factory is quite shaken following the most recent incident. In the packing section of the warehouse, a gruesome tragedy occurred concerning several hundred-pound pallets of canned tuna and Ms. Jackie Rose.

Apologies in advance for the more personal tone of this report, as it is one that I (Health Supervisor Hannah Lee) witnessed.

At approx. 5:10 p.m., a loud thud could be heard ringing throughout the factory. I heard the sound from my office, and as if acting as one, nearly a hundred heads swiveled in the direction of the warehouse building. It didn't take long for the screaming to start. As I made my way to the warehouse floor, one worker ran past me and stopped at the phone hanging from the wall near the entrance of the warehouse.

Her face was gray, and she was sobbing.

As I continued in the direction that she came from, I could make out the words "crushed" and "pulp" and steeled myself as I rounded the corner to where a crowd of workers had gathered. Another employee smashed the emergency stop button, and I remember hearing a loud buzz followed by the hydraulics release as the mechanical arm that stacked tuna pallets ground to a halt.

The sound covered the soft yelp I couldn't contain when I saw Ms. Jackie Rose, unconscious. Cans of open tuna and wooden pallets were shattered, their contents spilled around her. The air smelled of blood and something else, fetid and hot. I suspect Ms. Rose may have relieved herself, but the mess... It could not be ascertained.

I looked up, pulling my eyes from her still form and the undefined liquids and chunks surrounding her. One pile of tuna pallets was significantly shorter than the rest. It appears that they had toppled off the highest point, and fell to the ground below, crushing poor Ms. Rose underneath.

Employees had left her where she fell, the damage apparent. She was not pinned—there wasn't anything to drag her out from under. Both of her legs had been... Well, to use a perhaps unprofessional term... Exploded under the impact. There were no limbs to save.

When Ms. Rose was carted away, she was still alive. Workers who witnessed the accident were sent home for the day.

As I accompanied the medical professionals and Ms. Rose to the parking lot, I couldn't help but notice Mr. Barnes' truck in his parking space. He had not materialized during the incident, and when I went to inform him about the setback in the warehouse, he was not in his office either.

The hospital should provide an update on Ms. Rose's status when she exits surgery.

End incident report.

***

Incident Report #1066

3/2/1998, 4:00 p.m.

Customer complaint resulting in temporary factory shutdown. In-spection requested

In something of an unusual instance today, I wanted to make sure an official report was made regarding the customer complaint that came straight into our factory. I don't log all the complaints, but this one seemed to require a deeper investigation into the factory that will affect operations for at least half a day.

This week, I was pulling double duty of a secretarial shift and answered a phone call concerning a customer whose name I shall not disclose. We take our complaints seriously here at the cannery, but I must admit this sounded almost too absurd at first to believe.

The customer claims that upon opening a can of tuna for her son's lunch, she was appalled at what she found within.

A clump of hair, wound into a knot. Thick. Blonde.

She claimed she found "a significant amount of it", taking up nearly a third of the space in the can.

I asked for her address and phone number so the company could reach out to her for further information. We've been told not to apologize when dealing with direct complaints until it is verified that our factory and company is responsible, but in this instance, I couldn't help but offer a "sorry" as we hung up the phone. She told me she had tracked the numbers on the product to us.

I began an investigation to determine the source by tracing back the dates and lot numbers. The date of the incident likely took place on the 10th of February. I questioned the workers who were in proximity to the tuna pre-canning and was able to track down all but one employee.

A Ms. Jessica Rothridge has since turned in her intent to quit and has not been on the premises since.

None of the contacted employees had any information regarding the incident.

I'm contemplating putting in a request for a potential recall of this lot, but unsure of how to proceed. There's no way to know if this is an isolated incident or not.

I called Mr. Barnes with my concerns and he hand-waived the situation away. I suppose my answer is there. It doesn't sit right, but I have no other leads. I'll file this away for now.

End incident report.

***

Update to Incident Report #1060
  3/3/1998, 2:15 p.m.
  Deceased party: Jackie Rose

The hospital has just called to inform us that Ms. Jackie Rose has unfortunately passed away from her injuries.

End incident report.

***

Additional Update to Incident Report #1060
  3/4/1998, 1:00 p.m.
  Deceased party: Jackie Rose

I feel obligated to report more details concerning this event.

Yesterday, I was overwhelmed by the news. We've had injuries in the past at this location, but never a fatality. And never—*never*—anything as gruesome and violent as what occurred that day.

In thinking about what happened on the afternoon of Ms. Rose's accident, I remembered something I didn't think necessary to record at the time. But upon hearing that she passed away, I've been turning the event over in my mind, even though it makes my stomach churn at the same speed.

Seeing the details over and over—the smashed legs and bits of her everywhere, intermingled with the tuna—started calling forth a surge of bile. But as the contents of my stomach almost breached my chest, a part of the memory emerged to push it back down.

I can hear it clearly: the sound of the emergency door of the warehouse, near the back and out of sight, opening and closing shut. There was a brief burst of an alarm, quickly terminated. Intentional.

Not many people have access to the emergency alarm system.

I don't know... My mind is racing, and I just can't think about this anymore.

End incident report.

***

Incident Report #1068
   3/8/1998, 2:10 p.m.
   Customer complaint resulting in temporary factory shutdown. Inspection requested.

It's happened again. Another angry mother calling about a contaminated tuna can. She was so angry she could barely explain, but I think I heard enough. Traced the lot back to the same production run as the previous complaint concerning the hair in the tuna can.

Not hair this time though...a tooth. Bloodied at the stump. The customer didn't realize it until she broke her own tooth biting into her sandwich.

Considering that this is the second call about this batch, there's no way we can pawn off responsibility to the cheese or mayonnaise or bread or whatever else she put on her sandwich.

I called all the employees on shift that day. The 10th of February. Tried to call Jessica Rothridge, the worker who quit, but no answer at her home either. Nothing is sitting right in my stomach.

I pulled an employee file on her, "Terminated" stamped on the front in red, bold ink. Found a picture paperclipped to her resume. Long blonde hair, pulled back. A smile on her face.

Not "quit", but "terminated"...

I began to wonder by whom.

End incident report.

***

Incident Report #1070
  3/10/1998, 5:10 p.m.

Nothing has happened today... Yet. But I needed a place to document what I just overheard.

I walked past Mr. Barnes' office, hoping to clue him in on this horrible pattern of events. We've never experienced this many accidents in such quick succession. I'm beginning to worry that we're cursed.

We're running through incident numbers like lottery numbers.

I raised my fist to knock on his office door.

I heard him shout. A curse, a slur I don't dare recreate here in this capacity.

But then more. Half a conversation over the phone, I think.

He growled. I heard it, low in his throat with my ear pressed against the door. Then he spoke, words uttered through the snarl of a mouth.

"I'll get it shut down, I promise," he said. And I wondered if he meant the factory. Knew he did but didn't understand what or why. The accidents? Or the whole factory itself?

"I didn't want this fucking responsibility in the first place, Carl," he continued. "Who even eats canned tuna anymore, anyways?"

I was afraid to keep listening, didn't want to be caught. Felt the dropping of my stomach as I pressed my ear harder against the door, confirming that I was learning privileged information.

"Look," he said, and I could hear his meaty hand hit the desk. "I don't want it to fail. Can't have that stain on my record, you know? I promise this will work." A pause, then: "I'll get it done."

The sound of the phone hanging up and my nerves must have too because I turned away from that door and tiptoed back downstairs.

In that moment I felt fear trickle through my blood and vibrate my bones. Mr. Barnes was never the most caring man, but he's clearly up to something and my gut and mind just keep shaking hands, in agreement that it's something to do with all of these incidents at the factory.

I checked the date—the 10th of March... And that's when I remembered Mr. Barnes was always here for site visits on the 10th.

My mind began swirling at the thought of Mr. Barnes being here on the date of the contaminated lots. I wondered if he had something to do with the missing employee and what looked like the ball of her hair in a can of tuna, a tooth in another.

I've been writing these reports and it just occurred to me that I don't even know who's reading them. I place them in Mr. Barnes' box each day, and each day the box is emptied.

With so many things going on, and so many nothings being done about it... I can't help but feel like no one is listening.

I'll hold off submitting this at any rate. Not sure who to even file these thoughts with.

***

Incident Report #1071
  3/11/1998, 4:40 p.m.
  Injury resulting in death
  Deceased party: Malcolm Anderson

I don't even know where to begin. I don't even know why I'm writing this report, because it's clear my documentation isn't resulting in anything.

Today... Today Mr. Malcolm Anderson passed away. Not even just passed away—that's too peaceful for what happened.

He didn't deserve it. None of the injured so far has deserved it, but Mr. Anderson...

Such an indignity. And so horrible to see.

Another equipment malfunction. I have no clue how it could have been anything but intentional given the circumstances. The machine responsible for cutting the metal loosened, or rather, someone loosened the bolts.

It swung around and around the facility, the workers screaming at it spun and spun, promising a death it delivered with a cold viciousness. I ran to the sound of screams and halted in the doorway when I saw the machine whirling its sharp threats around the room, reckless blades spinning.

Mr. Anderson... Malcolm... God, my friend... He ran toward the door but not fast enough.

The metal decapitated him in one fell swoop.

The factory will be closed until further notice. The investigators have been here trying to discern what went wrong. I don't know why this one finally called the safety of this place into question.

Whoever did this took a wrong step. Didn't leave much room for the word "accident".

I'm about to leave for the day, or week, or whatever is left, but I wanted to at least put this into words before I go.

Malcolm was sweet. And from everything I could tell, so were Matalie, and Jackie, and Percy, and Jessica (she still hasn't been found, save for the hair and tooth I assume to be hers). To think that they, and probably countless others, have suffered at the hands of this factory.

This factory and its puppeteer.

Mr. Barnes, that son of a bitch.

I'm going to the police. I'm going to his office. Need to find those incident reports so I can turn them over to actual human eyes that will bear witness to whatever he's done for whatever his reasoning is.

I'm going to...

I've sat here for five minutes. Building the courage. I'm so scared to do what I have to do. I have a partner and kids and I'm just a health supervisor supposed to be dealing with the occasional severed finger or overused sick leave or possible contamination of rotten tuna.

But I need to. I will—

Dammit. Footsteps. I thought I was the only one here.

I waited it out. Didn't want to type for fear they'd hear the keyboard. They walked around. The sound of a single pair of heavy boots.

I wonder why Mr. Barnes is doing this. I play the phone call over in my head that I overheard. Get the factory to close. No stain on his record. Didn't want the responsibility.

That bastard. Trying to make it look like malfunctioning equipment instead of something that falls on his shoulders. He took it too far though. Didn't know enough about how the machinery works here to keep up the façade of accidents.

I wonder who else knows. Maybe Jessica saw him. That's why she's missing.

The pieces fall into place.

He'll pay. I'm going now to his office.

I'll make this right, I promise. I'll—

***

This final incident report was found still in the typewriter, next to Hannah Lee's body. She was dead by blunt force trauma to the back of her head.

Authorities were alerted to an emergency at the Shover's Valley Cannery when a plume of smoke enveloped the skyline. A fire, which started in the warehouse, was knocked back by firefighters before it consumed the main building.

Authorities suspect Mr. Kevin Barnes, the owner and manager of Shover's Valley Cannery, of starting the fire and is responsible for the injuries and deaths contained in this investigative report.

It appears Mr. Barnes planned to collect insurance on the terms of "malfunctioning equipment". Documents were found outlining suits against the various manufacturers of the equipment utilized by the factory. When Mr. Barnes realized his final "accident" would not yield the perception of a malfunction, but rather clear, intentional sabotage, he attempted to destroy all evidence of his involvement.

He has failed. His attempt cost Mrs. Lee her life. She is survived by her partner and two children.

If you have any information about Kevin Barnes and his whereabouts, please contact the Shover's Valley police department.

Chapter 12
The Thickest Soup You've Got

A fork in the road. Okay. But I have this map and I can see just off the edge of where the coverage ends a little "X" written in red, in the margin to the right of this path.

Right it is.

I've been in this car for what feels like hours, pushing away, but always relenting to highway hypnosis. The kind that sends you into that deeper state of being where you aren't really sure what you are and where you're at and if what you're even looking at is road anymore.

Tried to keep my eyes peeled as much as I could for a sign that I should exit.

I think this is it. This fork in the road, where my tiny VW Bug is idling. No other cars in sight or even the barest hint of civilization except this road, which means someone was out here paving.

And that red "X" on the map.

Foot off the brake, my car rumbles forward and I head to the right. Trees blur in my peripheral, and I'm headed into the forest deep. Such a rapid pace, those trees come and go and seem to curl over the road behind me.

I wonder if they're hiding my descent.

What am I even descending into?

I woke up in my VW, tank full of gas, but a head empty of thoughts. It felt like someone had plucked my car and set me on a track, at the starting line for a race I still can't remember signing up for. I don't know how I got there, struggle to remember who I am. The reflection in the rearview doesn't offer answers. All I can see is a girl with a messy mop of brown hair, worried hazel eyes the color of split pea soup, browning around the rim, and a stomach full of something I don't remember eating.

I give a little burp, trying to see if I could conjure up some flavor or remnant of the last meal I ate. Nothing tastes right though. Just something grainy, the hints of herbs I can't identify.

No answers, but a lot more questions.

Things start to flood back once I take that right turn. I remember who I am. Misaki. Twenty-five years old and in the middle of a road trip to experience life in ways I've never been able to before. Or at least, that was the plan.

All I had was a map sent from an ex. I hadn't heard from him in so long, and maybe I should have questioned his letter more than I did. But there was a warmth emanating from that envelope, one that reminded me of where I'd been and what I wanted to do. Brian said in his note that I needed to live a little, something he'd always criticized me for in the heyday of our relationship. I can almost see his heart-shaped lips spilling those words from his mouth as he said it.

In that moment, reading those words, I felt that damnation I'd held inside for so much of my life. A choir of "Stop being such a square" or "Jeez, let loose, Misaki," rattled through my brain. But there those words were, held up against the admonishments of my parents who urged me to keep a quiet, steady life. To have ambitions that would lead to my financial success. I was a walking, talking cliché, and I never had the guts to break free from those binds.

Those words written by Brian, two years my ex, had moved me in a way that all of my adult years had failed to do. I didn't know why, but it was almost like I could hear that map and the unknown destination calling to me.

I showed my new partner what he'd written, and she just shook her head. Edie didn't much like to talk about Brian, and I didn't blame her with all the less-than-kind things I had to say about him and our relationship. She wasn't too happy at all when I said I wanted to follow the map. She'd spent so long boxed in by my parents' assessment of her. Her first issue: she was a girl, and my parents, ever the traditionalists, couldn't bear the thought. Once she recognized that she could win them over by agreeing with their ambitions for me, I realized just how bound by their expectations she was. An unwilling slave in their pursuits for the very best for me.

So, I told Edie, "Screw it." And I showed her that map and the words of an ex she never met but always hated. Something fundamental in me shifted then.

Still, my stomach flips when I remember the disappointment in her eyes and voice. I remember our fight. The way I grabbed this map and a suitcase and said I'd be back in a week. My harsh words that the only thing holding me back was her. I knew it was a lie, but I said it anyway. Edie told me not to expect her to still be there when I returned.

But now, I don't even know how to return, only know this road and my car and the emotions I'm drenched in.

The road continues, and my mind races, searching for familiarity. I can't help but shake the déjà vu I'm feeling as my car jostles over rocks and bumps in the road. Not only that I've been here before, but that I've been here more times than I can ever dream of recalling.

I start to feel more like myself the deeper I get into the trees. Remember things about me. Good things, bad things, even the in-between things. I start to hate myself as I drive, and drive, away from a pretty damn good life toward something that only guaranteed a mystery. A hope. I contemplate turning the wheel around and heading back in the other direction.

Back to comfort. Back to stability.

It does sound quite nice—

A sharp pain strikes my skull and my eyes blur as I try to keep my vision on the road before me. Noise, loud and sharp like static in between my ears, reverberates like someone's trying to blow a balloon up inside my head.

It feels like someone screaming obscenities in my face, punctuating a denial of my own ability to think, to make decisions. The deafening anger consumes, and I know I can't turn this car around.

As suddenly as it starts, it's over.

A calm stillness as whatever unidentifiable thing that is now a part of me takes control and gets its way.

There's that highway deep sleep again. The trees are like a mobile above my bed, sending me into this state where I can do nothing but keep the wheel straight and my foot on the gas.

It won't let me think. Won't leave me be. My mind takes the backseat to a pop-up book of images, things I don't remember ever seeing before, but I can recall all the same.

Flashes of flesh. The echoes of viscous swamp between my toes. A stench that echoes in my brain, recalling being the smell of my own skin boiling.

A deep voice telling someone—something that it's not ready. Screaming out one word that I wish I could obey.

"Stop." Memories of something listening, scooping me from the lava I live in.

That voice, otherworldly, spoken through a vat of molasses and bones, rattling and rumbling in my head, shakes more cobwebs loose.

I notice my skin has that heavy heat to it, like day-old sunburn. I realize just how red and irritated my hands look, gripping the steering wheel.

There are worries in my mind that I can't bear, but all I can do is drive and drive and hope not to trigger another onslaught of visceral and disturbing images that feel so much like memories.

I drive and wait to see where the road takes me.

***

The clock in my car doesn't work. I don't have a phone, either, lost somewhere with my ability to turn this car around. I can only tell how much time has passed by the way the sun has begun to dip under the canopy of trees. It's right in my line of sight, bright like a bastard ball of lightning flashing as it dips between the limbs of trees. Driving at this time of day always feels dangerous, like any errant beam of light in your eyes could spell your death at a missed obstacle or turn or oncoming car.

It's a damn good thing there haven't been many of those to contend with. The road has been almost a straight line, and I haven't seen another car at all. Not since I woke up in this vessel of confusion.

There's a familiarity in my gut as the sun sets and the road narrows. It isn't long after that the shape of a wooden cabin makes its way onto the horizon.

I don't even hesitate as I turn my car onto the path leading to the building. Rocks and sticks crumble and churn under the wheels of my car. I slow to a stop.

Reaching over to my passenger front seat, I grab the map with the red "X" marked in the margins.

I know I am here, at this cross marked the color of an angry boil.

This cabin, at the end of the map, down a road that feels like it shouldn't exist.

I exit the car, the slamming of my door loud in the silent woods.

I reach the door, and a small etching in the wood catches my eyes. I raise my hand, feeling the carvings in the wood. I see letters—NO—and then a long scratch in the wood like the writer's hand was ripped from its task.

Phantom sensations of a slimy hand on my own drill my mind, and I wonder if I was the author of the message.

I'm not allowed to contemplate for much longer, as a force propels me forward. I push open the door, much lighter than I would have expected for wood as thick as it appeared. The creak of the hinges is long, tearing throughout the house like a zigzagging fly.

"Hello?" I call out, finding nothing living beyond the front door.

Inside the cabin, the air is moist, thick with humidity that smells like a sauna. The odor is nothing short of the scent I'd expect from people gathered in a hot room, their bodies exuding the ichor of a rotted core.

I weave throughout the rooms. Most are empty, with what looks to be water-stained floorboards, and grimy wallpaper that curls from the wetness of the air.

My legs still refuse to take my own commands, following the call of something that has encroached on my being. Something that pulls me only forward and never back and only allows me to wonder where I'm going.

The center of the cabin, which seems to sprawl far beyond the appearance of its size, is soon upon me. There's a door, and from behind it, I can hear a chattering. There's a voice—high-pitched, like an insect of a woman crying out. And beyond that, a deeper, throatier moan that passes for vocalization.

My heart stutters when I recognize it as the voice that yelled "Stop" in my faint memories of a life I'm told I lived, but remains distant and just out of reach.

The door swings open.

Two heads that don't look like heads, can't be heads, but are because there are eyes and mouths with crooked lips. Those lips are creeping open into a smile that reveals toothless gums, the color of soil. I hope this means they won't eat me with nothing to chew my sinew and skin, but I am not absolved of my fears when they lick their lips with tongues that are black and marked with pustules that dot the terrain like stars on the night sky.

"She's back," the smaller one says. She claps her hands.

"She's early," the deep voice says.

They wear tattered clothes, bits of burlap are fashioned into something that approaches the jacket a chef might wear in a fancy kitchen. The clothes cover slimy skin, folds of what almost looks like scales buckling beneath one another flowing from arms and legs revealed by the open slips of their suits.

In front of them is a pot of enormous proportions. Black, pocked metal, curved into a cauldron of sorts that approaches the size of a jacuzzi stares at me, its open center filled with a bubbling, thick, broth with unidentifiable contents.

"You've had time to...stew?" the small one asks.

I can't answer, can only respond with the questions I try to force from my lips but come as a mush of nonsensical grumbling noises. My mouth has followed the path of my legs—no longer under my control.

"Hush," the large creature says. "I can sense that you have been tenderized, but we will only know when you percolate in the depths of our bowls."

The high-pitched voice cackles, and the smaller creature rubs her stomach. "And the depth of our bowels."

She slides her body to a rack of utensils and stirs the contents of the pot in front of her. Her arms seem to stretch to impossible lengths to cover the full rotation of the comically sized pot.

The creature with the deeper voice smacks the backside of her head. "We do this not for our own satiation. But for the children below. You know this, Talsia."

Talsia turns something an approximate shade of red as she stirs. "Just a jest, Varnoc."

This scene before me—this horrifying scene of otherworldly creatures preparing a soup that I can only assume I am the missing ingredient for—has rendered me still. Not that I could move or speak if I wanted to, but my mind can't comprehend what hell I've stumbled into in this cabin.

The creature called Varnoc speaks again. "We know you are confused, Misaki. You were last time, as well. And, almost irreconcilably so the time before that. We've explained before your role in this all. That you will be served as a meal to our children below, but only once your flavors properly season the soup."

Talsia approaches me, and I am still rooted in my spot, my feet affixed to the ground as if with glue, my lips sealed by the same. "I'm going to undress you now. And then you'll take your place in the vat." She is gentle as she removes my flannel shirt and jeans, though with an air of impatience. Her nails brush my naked skin, though she is careful not to draw blood.

Once my clothes are folded on a shelf beside the vat, Varnoc snaps his fingers and my legs begin to move once more against my will. I walk right up to the edge of the vat, my toes curling over the red-hot sides, burning blisters into my feet.

"We thank you for this chance to assess you once more." Another snap, and my knees bend a little as I jump into the vat. As my feet slap against the bubbling liquid, I'm assaulted by memories that span my lifetime. Childhood disappointments, bad breakups, graduations, learning to drive, my parents divorcing, the death of my cat... It all spins together in a violent whirl, surging forward just like the soup I am sitting in frothing at the edges of my mind.

"Your fifth assessment now, Misaki. We see that you are offering more of your experiences."

More memories, some insignificant. The snapping of a pencil in my hand, falling off a swing, my first swim in the ocean...

"These are good. Deeper. Essences of you."

Varnoc continues to speak of the things I recall, pulled from my pores and entering the broth. The liquid is hot, and I worry my skin will slough off my bones. I can feel blisters on the bottoms of my feet.

"Next time, we will have you write a letter to the next offering. Last time you were here, you cried out a name. Edie, I think. Perhaps you can think of what she means to you and how you can call her to us on the next drive up here. We are close, but I think we can go deeper still. Drink up," he says. The soup enters my mouth, chugging down my throat and coiling in my intestines. "Let it seep within and cull you forth. We are excited to taste the thickest soup you've got."

Talsia's eyes flash a fire as she licks her lips again. "We send you off once more and hope that you return with a mind more tenderized. The open road casts a spell that frees you from more than you will ever know."

Varnoc's fingers, snarled and wet, snap once more, and the bubbling inside the vat disappears with my consciousness.

***

I've done this before, haven't I? If I was reading my own life story, I bet I could backtrack about ten pages or so and find this all written out already.

Wake up inside the VW Bug. Strange taste in my mouth. Brown hair, green eyes. Map in my lap. Hands shaking.

Maybe shaking more than before.

A stomach so full it's ready to burst.

A mind so pulverized, every memory is a tender flash that's hidden beneath layers of meaty pulp.

My hands are not my own. They turn the key in the ignition. My feet hit the pedal and I accelerate down a road, cushioned by trees. I find a fork. I turn right.

My mind is filled with chaos. Voices from other planes of existence. Memories from a life I swear I've lived. Visions of the people I've loved. My family. Brian. Edie.

They must wonder where I am. I still do, too.

The road thins. The sun sets.

I scold myself for taking this path. For venturing out to explore this map, sent from an ex I don't speak to in search of what? Myself? Did I ever find her?

I'm exhausted. Like I've fought and lost this battle over and over. Like I've tried to turn the car around countless times, but couldn't. Like I tried to pull over to the side of the road. But I could do nothing but follow the path to what I now know exists at the end.

A cabin, small and unassuming.

A set of doors, lighter than I prepare for.

A room at the center of a cabin.

An unpleasant smell, like flesh submerged in viscous, boiling liquid. I know this is a familiar scent now.

More doors, ornate, pushed open by arms that are alien to me.

Two figures, shuddering with delight, arms stirring spoons in a vat. They tell me who they are, and I wonder if they ever tired of introducing themselves to strangers that are not so strange to them.

I scribble a note. Talsia places it next to the map I've taken inside, still clutched in my hands that feel numb from detachment.

To Edie, the envelope reads. Talsia sheaths my betrayal within.

A snap of fingers.

Clothes removed.

Varnoc's voice is deep, but lilts with excitement when he remarks how ready I am. That surely, this will create a soup thicker than he hoped for.

I think I hear the cries of the children below, mouths open and ready for the offering of me.

Toes grip the side of the vat. I contemplate giving one last push of resistance against my eventual demise, but my connection to my body is more tenuous than before. I wonder which nerves Varnoc puppeteers and how he does so while touching nothing.

I've looped this path more times than I know. Have kissed this pot with my feet, steeping in this stew.

It's time for something else. To break the loop. Do something new. Something I am sure has not happened yet, as my face has remained unmarred by this journey.

My lungs are unable to hold breath. The whole thing feels rather unceremonious without that final gasp of air.

I submerge my head, for the first time hearing the song of the soup I'll sleep in.

Clutched in her depths, I think she's beautiful.

About the Author

Nikki R. Leigh is a queer, forever-90s-kid wallowing in all things horror. When not writing horror fiction and poetry, she can be found creating custom horror-inspired toys, making comics, and hunting vintage paperbacks. She reads her stories to her partner and her cat, one of which gets scared very easily.

Nikki is the author of *Her Teeth, Like Waves*, and the short story collection *Lessons in Demoralization*. She also has stories published in *Dark Matter Magazine*, *The Book of Queer Saints*, Cemetery Gates' *A Woman Built By Man*, *Diet Riot: A Fatterpunk Anthology*, Dread Stone Press' *Field Notes from a Nightmare*, Ghost Orchid Press' *Chlorophobia*, and *Shredded: A Sports and Fitness Body Horror Anthology* among other publications.